A TASTE OF HONEY
and other stories

Michael B. Fletcher

A TASTE OF HONEY
and other stories

DOUBLE DRAGON

TABLE OF CONTENTS

Ink of Life
Love of Music
Soulsearcher
It Is As It Should Be
Horsenail
The Guard
One of a Kind
Out of Time
Pain
Promising Future

A Taste of Honey

'Them bees come outta nowhere. Soon as you open a bottle they're there. And vicious? If'n yer don't give 'em a sniff they'll sting.' He peered down at the young boy from beneath bushy eyebrows. 'Not that a youngster of your age should be drinking mead.

'When I were your age the best I could do was smell it. Closest I got fer many years. Wasn't till Mary, uh...' His voice trailed off and the boy, perched on the gnarled root at his feet, sighed and wriggled his numb bottom for a more comfortable seat.

'The bees, Grandfer.' His shrill voice broke the silence. 'You were talkin' 'bout the bees.'

'Uh, Chad, don't interrupt,' he puffed on a blackened pipe, 'I were thinking.'

'Yes Grandfer, I know.' The boy looked into the thick foliage above his head, trying to estimate where the sun had moved to on this still afternoon.

The day was hot, full of the drone of insects and the gradual slowdown of growth as living things readied themselves for the cooler evening. The temptation to settle and doze was great and Chad found his Grandfather's voice soporific.

A burdened bee slowly buzzed through the air, taking a detour around the solid figure blocking its way. Two pairs of eyes followed its progress until it circled once, twice and disappeared into the bee skep firmly wedged at the base of the ancient tree.

'Them,' came Grandfer's voice as he gestured with his pipe. 'Them's what makes the honey. And where the mead comes from. Them's what brought my Mary to her ruin.'

'Grandfer?' Chad wriggled excitedly as he realised he might finally learn what had happened to his mother, an unseen, unspoken influence in his life.

'Uh,' the old man huffed as he eyed his grandson settling in for an explanation. 'S'pose it's time yer knew, knew 'bout yer Ma and what she was like.

'Pretty as a picture. Hair like yours only fluffier, bouncier, stretching like wisps of cloud as she played. She was happy here, 'specially before she knew boys.' He slowly shook his grey head. 'But one thing she liked, always liked, were bees and their honey.'

As if to emphasize his words, another bee buzzed past towards the dark skep only distinguishable from the gnarled tree roots by its conical shape.

'Mead!' He jabbed his pipe stem at the hive. 'Nice in moderation, 'specially on a cold night. But too much...' His voice faded away.

'Grandfer?' Chad's call echoed plaintively.

'Uh, yes, mead. But if it weren't fer it Mary wouldn't have met him and you wouldn't be here.'

'Me? Yer talkin' 'bout my Pa? I have a Pa?'

'Hush, let me tell the story. Course yer have a Pa. No need to rush on a day like today.' He rubbed a hand through Chad's untidy dark hair.

'Group of travellers came through town, a rare enough event. So we gave 'em hospitality, food and drink. And they stayed for a week. Little did we know what that would bring. Handsome devil he was, too. Too much fer a country girl like me daughter to resist. Then they left. Left me and my Mary. And then,' he smiled sadly at Chad, 'you made yer presence known.

'Too late fer us to do anything 'bout it. Too late to take down the man responsible. Too late fer Mary.

'Course I were too stubborn to take notice of what it was doing to my Mary, jest blamed everyone fer what had happened. Then you arrived.' He pushed his booted foot through the detritus at his feet.

'Then why isn't my Ma here? Why did she go and leave me?' Chad's eyes glistened blackly at his grandfather through the tree's shadow.

'Ah,' the old man replied, the sound dragging slowly out of his mouth as he looked down at the skep. 'I suppose I should blame them bees for it was their mead thet took yer Ma. She turned to it more 'n more as you grew, leaving me to raise you as best as I could. Fer she weren't a fit mother, she could hardly look after herself let alone a baby.'

'But I like honey, Grandfer. I've never had mead. How could mead make her a bad Ma? Make her want to leave me?'

'No, Chad,' he smiled at his grandson, 'she didn't want to leave you, she jest had some mighty issues to deal with and you didn't figure in them.'

'Then, then…' Chad struggled with his words, 'why, if'n you blame them bees and… don't keep them skeps for more'n a season or two - is that one still there?' He pointed to the age-darkened skep wedged firmly amongst the tree roots. 'Never had the honey from it neither.'

'No matter, boy!' he snapped. 'We were talking about yer Ma, not her hive. No,' he squinted into the thick leaves above his head, 'we were talking 'bout my Mary.

'Anyhow, time we were moving. Getting' dark.' He shifted his bulk from where he leant against the gnarled trunk.

'Grandfer,' whined the boy.

9

He paused, took a suck at a dead pipe and sighed. 'Always felt closest to Mary here. Her tree, her hive and now you. Still, enough maudlin talk. We best be off, that's if you want yer supper. C'mon, lad.'

'Not hungry. So what happened to her, Grandfer. What happened?'

'Dammit boy, can't you leave well-enough alone?' he said, striding away from the tree.

'You promised!'

The old man swung around to see the tableau of the tree, the skep and his grandson silhouetted against a setting sun. 'Ah hell, Chad, just come away from there. We've gotta go now that it's getting dark.'

'You mean she's dead, don't you?'

'Ah Chad,' he coughed, wiping a sleeve across his eyes. 'Come 'ere,' he crouched on his haunches and held out his arms to his grandson. 'All I can say is that yer Ma left us fer a better place, she'll never be coming back, but she'll always be watching over you.

'We've got each other, still got each other.'

The meal was a sombre affair. Chad's grandfather refused to divulge any more about his mother and the plain meal felt like sawdust on his tongue.

That night he lay in his narrow bed, mind roiling with the events of the day. His mother's face drifted across his mind, sad eyes under a cloud of dark hair. He could feel her trying to calm him, comfort his worries, give him some peace. But then a taste began to override the sour meal, a sweetness on the tip of his tongue, the taste of honey.

He tossed and turned as the taste filled his mind, refused to let him sleep, reminding him of a dark place where the bees buzzed. Suddenly he was there, back to the tree, darker now in the moon-lit night. He looked around but he was alone, no sound and no other presence.

Chad strained his ears as he heard a vague hum from the base of that ancient tree. His breath caught in his throat as he stumbled his way across the tangled roots towards the source of the noise. His knees banged harshly on rough ground as he reached out to touch the unnatural shape outlined against a glimmer of moonlight.

An increased humming reacted to his touch as his palms caressed the abraded conical shape. A drift of honey reached his nose, mirroring the taste still in his mouth. In that moment he felt a close connection to a person he never knew but yet had had such an influence in his life. Chad rubbed his face on the skep's surface, wanting to prolong the feeling, not wanting to break the connection. But then he felt the structure move and lift from its position amongst the roots of the ancient tree.

A gush of honey flooded out, littered with sleepy bees as the skep fell onto its side. The boy put a wondering finger in the sticky mess before sucking off the honey. At that moment a shaft of light from the angled moon shone onto the fallen hive, highlighting the edges of the broken honeycomb and the shadows. The light glistening off a honey-covered surface attracted his attention. He looked closer, seeing a bony structure white in the dark, sharp ridges above two black holes, gaping teeth below. The breath stopped in his throat and he reached an inquiring finger to brush away the flow of still bees and understand what he was seeing.

He pushed back onto his heels and scrabbled to his feet, a sticky hand pressed to his mouth. *No!* his mind screamed, *No!*

He sat upright in his bed, gasping, looking wildly around his familiar room. *Just a dream,* he thought, *just a dream.* His heart rate slowed as he lay back down, letting his dream fade before sleep claimed him.

Even as he drifted off, he pushed a thumb into his mouth and snuggled down to where not even the taste of fresh honey roused him out of what waited for him in the coming of the day. For he knew he would be drawn to the hive where his Ma was waiting.

Attraction

There was a light on in the empty room. Insects attracted by the light entered through the door and competed for its illumination until the room was empty again. Daylight revealed a scatter of wings and legs, victims of the lure of its beam. The pile of moth parts grew nightly. A bat blundered in after a meal; its bones added to the pile. Still the light shone. Several owls added their carcasses until the floor became a mat of desiccated body parts and bones.

A traveller, noticing the light, followed the beam, blundering through rough countryside until forced to camp and wait until morning.

He found the light in an empty one-roomed dwelling. It hung glowing from a short cord with no obvious power source. Hairs rose on the back of his neck as he crunched through the carpet of material covering the floor. He quickly left.

The light seemed more obvious the next night, filtering through the undergrowth to find the traveller's eye. He shifted until it became hidden but he saw its presence by a glow on nearby bushes. He shut his eyes and tried for sleep. His mind was overactive. Was the light growing in brilliance? Trying to attract him? Sleep eluded him.

Next day he re-entered the empty room and found no trace of his footprints on the floor. He shook his head and turned on his heel. There was no sign of the owner.

The dull, gloomy day added to his mood as he continued on his way, pondering the mystery of a light that never went out. Why was it left on? What was its power source? He forgot his bearings as he walked, then realised the clouds had become oppressive.

He set up camp, keen to make up for an interrupted sleep the previous night. A flicker crossed his eyes as he settled. A glow lit the low clouds.

'Hell!' He picked up a fallen branch and strode towards the beacon.

He pushed open the door. A huge moth flew past and circled into the light, creating a brief flash. A cascade of legs and wings floated to the floor.

'That's it!' He gritted his teeth, stepped forward and swung the branch at the light - and missed.

The glare was dazzling, seemingly brighter than before.

He shielded his eyes withone hand and stepped closer, feet crunching on bones.

Another swing. Another miss.

He dropped the branch and snatched at the light, determined to pull it down and extinguish it.

A flash blinded him as a sharp pain traversed his body.

He knew no more.

A cascade of bones hit the floor and the light grew stronger.

14

An Unlikely Hero

The earth erupted in a mass of rocks and soil, startling the sheep grazing on the hillside. They scattered, bleating their panic as a series of thumps shook the ground.

'What!' exclaimed Claiyt, lifting his sleep-filled head from the gnarled tree trunk. His eyes widened at seeing the rocks rolling down the hill. 'Shit, Jedra!' he screeched, pulling at his wisp of a beard. 'Yer gotta see this!'

'Huh?' A tall skinny youth staggered to his feet and caught sight of the sheep disappearing down a dried watercourse. 'The blood-cursed sheep are running off and you're s'posed to be on watch. We'll cop it from the Elders if any go missing.'

'Did yer hear it, Jedra!' yelled Claiyt, grabbing at his friend's woollen tunic. 'Did yer?'

'Sheep. That's what we've gotta worry about. Sheep, not whatever you've been dreaming. Come on or as sure as hell every brigand in Dravia will be eating roast mutton.' Jedra bent down to pick up his water bottle, satchel and spear.

Claiyt glanced up to the site of the eruption puzzling at the wisps of steam rising into the blue sky before snatching his own belongings.

Rocks rattled from the hole near the summit of the hill. Metal clinked and an armoured head rose above the rim, metal-gloved hands focussing a set of bronze-rimmed oculars on the departing youths.

'Sendra!' The figure turned in a faint screech of metal. 'I think we may have been noticed by the overlanders.'

'Marcrem?' A similarly armoured figure appeared against a dark structure further down the hole.

'The Beasts, I think.'

'At once!'

Sendra turned and pushed a metal door, causing it to swing silently inwards, revealing a well-lit space. A drift of steam puffed from his concealed shoulder vents as he walked inside.

Marcrem continued to scan the countryside, fingers tapping a staccato rhythm on his metal sleeve.

He relaxed at the scrabble of bronze claws and a grim smile split the metal mask. Two four-legged beasts climbed past, steam filtering from their nostrils. 'Hold!' he snapped, arm held out. The creatures froze. 'Sendra, will they be able to track overlanders amongst those animals?'

'Sir, the olfactories are calibrated and the beasts will operate for over two hours until they need refuelling. I anticipate they'll return well before that.'

'The General will accept nothing less,' Marcrem growled. 'There must be no hint of our presence.' He dropped his arm and the waist-high forms, metallic teeth clashing, leapt from the hole before pounding down the hillside and out of sight, steam hissing from their bronze-coloured bodies.

Soon the screaming echoed.

'Disturbing reports, Elder Potriatis,' said a large man with greying beard and a swelling paunch his robes failed to conceal. 'A sentinel slaughtered. Sheep too. The wounds are consistent with wolves but the words of the survivor don't make sense.'

'Mmmm,' nodded the Elder as he considered the statesman's words. 'This is indeed worrying, Elder Sensesis.' He looked at the man sitting on the cushioned seat across the large marble-tiled room. 'Continue.'

Sensesis took a sip of wine from a blue glass. 'One Claiyt, a fit enough young man with fair training, reports a, uh, hill exploding in the middle of the day. This caused the sheep to scatter. Shortly thereafter they were set upon by two beasts best described as wolves of metal.'

'An exploding hill?' Elder Potriatis had an amused expression on his lined face. 'And wolves of metal? If it weren't so serious I'd think you were duping me.'

The large man sat forward. 'No, Potriatis, no. This Claiyt seemed certain of his facts even though he knew he might not be believed. And as for the wolves--my words, not his. But he spoke of the impossible metal beasts and steam.

'I sent him to the apothecary.'

'So, Sensesis.' The Elder ran a hand through his sparse grey hair. 'I think we should discuss this disturbing event in the Quorum.'

'I agree, Potraitis.' The large man stood. 'I shall make the necessary arrangements.'

'General,' Marcrem bent his head to the figure emerging out of the dark tunnel. 'We are in readiness.'

'Were you observed?' The metal head's piercing yellow eyes focussed on Marcrem, steam hissing from its mouth vent.

'Uncertain, sir. We believe two herders of, ah, sheep may have heard something, but the Beasts resolved that issue. They returned bloodied.'

17

'Hmm, no matter.' The General's head turned towards the night sky. 'I assume you've verified our position?'

'Sir,' replied Marcrem. 'We emerged in the hill two miles east of Dreverium, as calculated. The mountains of Atlasius are behind us, to the west. Aside from a dam or two there is little habitation to concern us.'

'Good. The locals should be easily overcome. The primitives cannot compete with our technology.' He paused, watching the far off twinkle of lights from Dreverium.

'What are your orders, General?'

'Continue as you are. We assemble and move the force out at first light. We need this land taken with a little spoilage as possible.' The figure looked at Marcrem. 'Go about your duties.'

'Sir.' Marcrem descended into the tunnel.

'Yes,' mused the leader. 'Our people will be most pleased. From famine to plenty, from sterile underground to the bountiful surface. Yes, most pleased.' He slipped armour-clad arms behind his back and looked up at the star-studded sky. 'To be the first in generations to observe those fabled objects.'

A figure crept up the slope, brown tunic melding into the drying grass and scattered bushes. He hid behind a boulder and peered into the darkness. A slight clink of metal, coupled with a hiss caught his attention. He crawled silently towards the bank of freshly disturbed soil then hesitated before picking up a small object from the ground and sliding it into his waist pouch, then creeping backwards across the hillside.

A hiss and the movement of a bulky bronzed-head above the bank made him freeze. He watched a white

18

cloud rise and dissipate before he continued moving to where a large water-filled dam filled the space between the hills. He paused for a moment then ran past the dam and along a track leading to Dreverium.

'No, you can't go it there!' came the loud voice of the guard. 'The Quorum's in session.'

'I must! I have news!'

'Claiyt, Elder Potriatis,' said Elder Sensesis, standing from amongst a group of robed men around the long wooden table. 'He's been back to the site of the massacre.'

'Bid him enter,' said the Elder. 'His words will surely aid our discussion.'

All the eyes focussed on the entrance to the meeting room as the youth walked hesitantly through the door. His tunic was dirty and mud covered his knees. Several of the Elders huffed at the breach of etiquette.

Elder Potraitis lifted an arm. 'Speak, young Claiyt. You have news of import?'

The youth's eyes flicked over the men of his city, the city of Dreverium before he reached into the pouch at his waist. He lifted a thin object about the length of his hand and placed it on the table in front the Elder. It clunked as it met the surface.

'Why, it's just a piece of bronze rod,' said a lined-face Elder.

'Is it?' Sensesis picked it up. 'It is weighty, very hard by its look, though bronze-coloured. What is it, Claiyt?'

The youth looked at the metal object. 'I don't know. It came from where the hill exploded, from where the beasts came that killed Jedra. I saw men there too. Metal men, same colour.'

The Elders started speaking amongst themselves until Sensesis raised his hand. 'Claiyt, repeat what you said.'

Claiyt took a large breath. 'I, uh, think it came from them. The metal men.'

'Huh.' A red-faced Elder of large build stood and pointed at the youth. 'You can't believe the ramblings of a beardless, untried youth. How can we make decisions of import based on such imaginings?'

'Elder Obstyentius!' Potraitis eyes flashed. 'Sit down and listen.' The man sat. 'Claiyt is the eye-witness to the massacre of the youth, Jedra, and almost an entire flock of sheep. His report is important.' He looked slowly around the table before signalling to Claiyt. 'Continue.'

And...' Claiyt's eyes widened, 'there... there was steam coming from them, like when water is boiling.'

Obstyentius jumped back to his feet. 'See, he is merely inventing a story.'

The table erupted into furious talk with the Elders shouting and waving their arms. Potraitis beckoned them to silence.

'It seems that we have a potential enemy using metals and of unknown power. A very real threat to the city.' He smiled sadly. 'What we do about it is open to discussion, but I believe we will have little time to decide.'

Claiyt waited until the talking died down before he cleared his throat. All eyes turned towards him. 'I... I think I might know of a way...'

The sun was rising from the sea, its rays lighting the dry hills, the olive-green vegetation and turning the walls of the city red. A caterpillar of bronze snaked its way along a dried watercourse towards the city of Dreverium.

20

Claiyt and a team of youths had left for the hills hours earlier, armed with digging equipment, the future of the city resting on their shoulders.

The stone walls of the city manned by squads of soldiers wearing tunics and armed with spears and bows, who were marching nervously to and fro along the parapets, looking into the hills that formed a backdrop to the city. Several patrols sent into those hills had not returned and rumours had spread of steam-producing metal creatures inhabiting them.

An eerie echoing wailing was the first indication of something amiss. Spears rattled and archers fitted arrows to their bows. A faint vibration was felt on the walls as the noise grew.

They focussed on a narrow road bisecting two hills.

A large figure, twice the height of a man, emerged and walked ponderously forward, stopping only three hundred feet away. A square metal head rested on armoured bronze-shoulders, the metal-plated body studded with rivets, legs and arms were metal pipes ending in gross feet and hands. Trickles of steam rose from hidden vents. A number of similar but smaller figures came up behind it. Flanking them were over a dozen four-footed, waist-high beasts, clashing metal teeth.

'I fear you were right, Potraitis,' murmured Obstyentius as he edged his way along the wall, horrified by what he was seeing.

'Whatever they are, I don't see how we can defeat them with our bows and spears,' said Potraitis to Sensesis.

The larger man gripped his friend's shoulder.

The huge metal figure began to move in a large hiss of steam, each step punctuated by a hideous squeal. It neared the city. The archers loosed a volley of arrows

21

which rattled off the armour to no effect. Each step took the figure closer to the massive timbered gates. Its army followed as the metal man broke through the barrier without effort. The four-footed beasts ran into the city square, biting and slashing, blood flying, men dying.

The terrified elders pressed against the stone battlements as the metal giant's head rotated their way, the body half turned, eye holes glowing redly. The mouth clanged open.

'Portraitis, may we meet in the afterlife,' said Sensesis.

'No, my friend,' said Potriatis. 'Move back. We must have hope.'

The screaming of the people melded with the thumps and bangs as the metal army continued its destruction.

Then a rumbling began causing the very wall to shiver. 'Look!' an archer shouted, arm pointing towards the road.

The ground appeared to ripple as first a trickle then a muddy wall of roiling water came thundering down the valley. The invading force stopped their killing to face the onslaught. The water rushed into the city walls, then funnelled through the opening in a powerful torrent.

'They've done it!' shouted Potraitis. 'They've done it!'

But the metal army stood firm, angled into the angry waters.

'It's not working!' said Sensesis, fingers gripping the stone.

A metal beast, bloodied cloth hanging from jaws, suddenly shivered as the water reached its neck. It disappeared in a rush of steam. One by one the remaining beasts disappeared under the torrent.

'This can't be!' The General's voice overcame the roar of the water. 'We have the right. Marcrem, stop it!'

Marcrem erupted in a plume of steam.

'Kill them! Kill them all!' The General screamed at the huge metal man. 'We must survive!'

The large figure placed a huge hand on the wall, gaze fixed on the cowering Elders. Ignoring the explosion of the General's body, it placed a second hand, then a massive foot onto the parapet and heaved upwards.

The defenceless men cowered away from the menacing bulk.

But the weight put strain on the wall already weakened by the deluge. It broke. Slowly, ponderously the creature fell backwards into the muddy waters, red eyes fastened on its prey.

A huge eruption of mud-coloured steam signalled its end.

***

'Legends are made, not born. And Talus, the bronze giant was not the hero of our legend. It was a man, merely a man. It was he who slew the giant.'

'Come, my children,' he said, 'and let us pass a leisure hour in storytelling. And our story shall be the education of our heroes. For heroes are created in the moment and not made as the myths would have us believe.

Elder Potraitis looked through the window at the young Elder Claiyt walking past in bright new robes of authority, before he turned back to the wide-eyed children facing him.

Ruff Deal

'My dear lady,' he gasped, body bending, back twisting, legs and arms shortening to accommodate his posture.

'Please tell me, my lady,' his tongue now hanging, drool spilling, 'what did I do?'

His next words became a bark as the muzzle formed and soft fur sprouted.

The witch smiled and picked up a leash.

The White Line

The chanting echoed down the tunnel, amplifying the buzzing in his head, driving away the disbelief that he could be here and now. Marcus grasped for tenuous memories, trying to hold them, but the noise broke through.

He cursed in a fluent but ancient language and dropped a hand to the hilt of his sword. He swung around, seeing the circle of light, knowing that he had to face this first; otherwise he could not be with her, his dark-haired lady.

His sandaled feet trod the gravelled way as had thousands before him. The light and the noise grew larger.

Marcus stood, blinking, feeling the bright sun and the harsh noise wash over him. Then he sought her face amongst the thousands that filled the rows of the stadium: one attractive face that wasn't baying for his blood, wasn't wanting him dead, that was filled with concern not fervour.

Yet this was his moment. He had a chance, a slim one at best, but a chance. Should he win and beat the Emperor's favourite, Crixus, he would be granted a boon. If events came out as he hoped he would gain her, Aemilia Secondia, and make her his wife.

A movement on the dry surface of the arena drew his attention. The man facing him was huge, bare chest covered in scars, round broken-nosed head covered in a helmet. He too wore a kilt secured by a leather belt, leather greaves protecting his shins. The sword he held seemed much larger than Marcus's.

The rules were simple. Kill or be killed. And Crixus had many kills to his name.

He remembered kneeling before the marble figure standing in the alcove of the temple, seeking the reason for his being.

Slowly, after an interminable time, a golden light had emanated from it, causing Marcus's body to pulse with health and vitality. He understood; the Augur had called him.

He had left in a daze, trying to make sense of the direction he had to take. Marcus ran his hand down the tunic, touching the belt holding the sword to his side as if feeling them for the first time. He had to see Aemilia, he thought as he easily found his way through the narrow streets of the city to her house, his mind giving him directions even though he couldn't remember having been that way before.

Marcus's broad chest heaved with exertion as he came to her house.

An ancient woman with suspicion in her eyes opened the door. She looked up at his tall form before nodding. 'You're back and wanting the Mistress?'

He held his instinct to push past, waiting for her to step aside. 'To the room on the right. That's where the Mistress be.'

'My thanks,' he said as he strode past. 'I know the way.' A thread of disquiet pulsed through him as he said the words. He rubbed his head as he entered the room.

A stream of sunlight lit a large, yellow-painted room, serving to highlight a dark-haired woman in a green tunic standing against an ochre coloured wall hanging. She smiled at him and hurried forward.

Marcus held out his arms before hesitating. The woman was so familiar, but yet?

'I knew you'd be returned. I'm so pleased to see you.' Her voice was soft and pleasing.

'As am I, Aemilia,' he said a frown appearing on his face.

'Oh.' She slowed and took his outstretched hands in hers. 'I'm sorry. I didn't realize you'd still be confused.'

'Confused, Aemilia?'

'It will come to you, my love. Let it happen.'

Marcus's mind was in a fog. He knew this woman intimately, yet it was as if he was meeting her for the first time. She led him to a leather-covered longue next to the wall hanging and they sat together.

'You have come from the Augur. Tell me what is required of you.'

'I... I have to fight to win you,' he mumbled.

'You are sure?' she asked, concern in her slanted dark eyes. She held his head between two soft hands, so close that strands of her curled black hair tickled his nose.

'Yes, Aemilia, and I'm sorry.'

'Don't be sorry. It is as the Augur requires, having returned your life. Now you have to follow that journey. Just tell me who it is and how I can help.'

Marcus pulled away. 'I am to best Crixus, the Emperor's favourite next day.'

'But he is unbeaten.' Her eyes welled with tears. 'This is the task you failed before. How can you be asked again?'

'Again?'

'Still you don't remember, beloved? Don't you recall your death?'

'N... no... I don't.'

27

'At the very least stay this night. Let us gather what comfort we may. Tomorrow will come soon enough.'

The large man flipped his huge sword from right to left hand, smiling as he did so. 'I'll give you a chance, fool. I'll fight with my other hand.' They circled, Marcus drew his sword and swung it experimentally, allowing himself to move with the blade and recognise the highly trained body he had.

'Do you want to keep your pretty head?' Crixus taunted as he moved, eyes fixed on his. 'For the lady that waits for you up there?' He jerked his head towards the stands, towards Aemilia.

Marcus gritted his teeth, dropped lower into a fighter's crouch and continued moving.

Crixus had lightning speed for such a big man and a strike that would fell an ox. His only chance would be to disable the man, get in quick blows that might weaken him - always with the thought that he'd done this before, had lost before.

The gladiator kept taunting him as they moved in the parody of a dance on the dusty surface. The roar of the crowd became the background. The eyes of his opponent were the only things he saw.

Marcus darted in, slashing at the man's torso. Crixus swung as he stepped back, the blade skimming his head. Marcus kept at it, using his speed to attack, trying to land a blow while avoiding being hit. Small cuts appeared on both of them, mixing with the sweat and dust.

The crowd roared as the fight progressed. Then Marcus dodged and feinted, slicing across Crixus's hamstring. The gladiator dropped to one knee, a hand scrabbling in the dirt, a serious expression on his face. The stakes had risen.

Marcus dashed in, sword raised. Crixus flung a handful of dirt, blinding Marcus as he swung at the man's head. He connected hard, feeling a glancing blow on his own body before he hit the ground.

The noise of the crowd ceased as he lay on the hard ground. He knew he had won.

Aemilia was there, cradling his head in her lap, weeping tears onto his face. He was calm, happy he had overcome such huge odds and won the right to his lady. *Why was she crying? All would be right now, wouldn't it?* Then the pain hit him, a sharp stab through his gut and he realised Crixus had won after all.

'No!' he yelled as she began to fade away, Aemilia's wide-eyed face breaking into wisps, drifting like fog, intangible and untouchable. His frantic hands fell through her thinning form as the world around him faded. 'Don't leave me like this!' Marcus screamed and slumped back, blocking out what was happening.

Slowly, noises began to register. The shouts of the spectators crying for blood were replaced by the hum of traffic, the clatter of trams, the calls of newspaper hawkers and the sounds of city life.

He lifted a tear-streaked face and looked over to the glass-topped table near him. 'Yes!' he hissed, 'there's enough to go back.' His shaking hand picked up the razor blade and clumsily moved the powder into a white line. He dropped the blade, grabbed a straw and sniffed up the drug. He didn't worry whether his wasted body could endure another dose, might die while he was gone; he only knew he had to return. 'Third time lucky, Aemilia.'

The Luddites

'Damn me, Ned, would yer look at thet,' he hissed. 'Two of 'em, bold as yer like. Don't thet prove it?'

'Doesn't mean anything really, Rob. Just means he's got connections with the Empire.' Ned pulled his thick coat tighter around his neck, wiped at his wispy beard and looked at the huddle of men behind him.

All were dressed in dark clothing, rugged up against the early morning chill and glancing up the long gloomy laneway overhung by fully leafed elms as if they expected something to come charging out of the darkness. They were fidgeting with their weapons and whispering to one another.

'Hisst, you lot. Settle! The stone eagles mean nothing. We have to do what we came for.' Ned touched Rob on the shoulder, pushed his cap down to his eyes and started walking down the laneway.

The scuff of boots and murmur of his companions gave him a modicum of comfort as they hurried down the dark corridor of trees. He kept his ears strained for the sound of the giant steam engines that Ludwig's Milling had installed, hoping that he had picked it correctly.

Ned began to relax as the only sound that broke the early morn was that of his men and the occasional clink of the iron bars they were carrying. It seemed the turncoat workers respected the Sabbath.

What a laugh, he thought, respecting God but not their fellow man and their families.

He had sussed out the grounds and workings of Ludwig's Milling by frequenting some of the taverns where the specialized technicians met after work. He realized they had been sworn to secrecy but it was amazing how much could be garnered after a few ales and pandering to their egos. The steam engineers in particular were so proud of their damned technology and had no concept of how it was ruining the life of the local workers.

He had tried legal channels but the Company had greased the pockets of too many politicians and lawyers. They gushed over the virtues of steam technology while the workers starved.

'No more,' Ned gritted his teeth as the trees thinned and the buildings hove into view. 'Quiet now,' he hissed, 'there's bound to be guards.'

The landscape was surreal, the buildings lying like sleeping whales with their steam breath spiralling into the crisp dawn air.

'There!' whispered Rob, pointing to a large building, its black shape looming in the slight mist. 'It's gotta be in there. See the trails of steam?'

'Hold up.' Ned stretched out an arm. 'There's guards.'

'No problem,' growled a voice from behind, 'we'll just crack their heads.'

'No, they've got helmets and they're carrying some kind of large gun. We'll have to be careful. Round to the back, quietly.'

Ned ushered the men around to the rear of the building while he couldn't help thinking the guards seemed unusually large as if they hadn't a fear in the world.

The building was of solid wood, freshly milled to fit without a gap. The door that they came to had a large sliding bolt with a steel padlock.

'Here, we'll use one of the bars and break it,' said Rob.

The crunch, then snap of the lock's fittings seemed unnaturally loud in the quiet of the dawn, only broken by the faint hiss of steam and the harsh breathing of the men.

It took two of them to push the door as if the building was reluctant to reveal its secrets.

Ned led his group in. The interior was softly lit by glowing fires near large metal cylinders near the centre of the building. He knew it housed machinery that was verging on the modern, taking the jobs of his fellow countrymen. He also knew what drove them.

'Spread out. Look for pipes; anything that seems warm where there's wheels set on them. That's what we're after.'

They moved through the vast space, the bulk of the strange forms becoming apparent. Huge round shapes squatted menacingly on either side, joined by thin spidery pipes–the hiss of their breath causing wavering columns of steam to rise into the blackness of the roof many feet above. They kept to a central pathway which crunched under their feet. Paired men split off and investigated every dark corridor as they walked until just Ned and Rob remained.

A large beam of metal, as thick as a man, blocked their way, attached to the rim of a massive pulley leading back to the bulky shapes they had passed. It was moving. In a ponderous yet smooth motion it slowly rose up, then down. Behind, into the dark, stretched rows of metal machines. Ned could see that they were in some way dependent on the huge beam for they seemed to be slowly ticking, spinning and juddering in concert.

'The men'll be waiting for the signal, Ned,' reminded Rob.

'Aye,' he gave a huge sigh, 'let's be at it then.'

He stepped up to the point where a huge pin locked the beam onto the pulley wheel and raised his metal bar.

With a quick flex of his muscles he crashed it onto the weakest point, causing a loud clang to reverberate. He was about to hit it again when he paused and listened. There was silence, no answering banging, anywhere. Ned turned to ask Rob, but he had disappeared.

'What?' He let the bar hang loosely from his hand as he strove to pierce the darkness to catch sight of his companions.

A burst of light dazzled him. He held a hand against his eyes until he saw figures coming towards him. They were huge, moving stiffly with a hiss of steam. Each of them held one of his men. Rob, a stunned look on his face, was the nearest, held immobile by two metal arms.

'Mr Ludd,' came a firm accented voice from the darkness, 'please release the bar or you will suffer the consequences.'

The bar dropped with a clang from nerveless fingers and he waited with resignation as the slow crunch of booted feet drew near.

'I have heard that you have been asking questions, many questions of my men when they have finished their duties and are taking relaxation in the local ale establishments.' The voice was thick and foreign. 'You must think me, Ferdinand Ludwig, an imbecile not to have noticed.'

The tall man now stood in front of him, the light from a lamp silhouetting his head. 'And then you think I will allow you and your men to enter a strictly forbidden area and destroy the machinery created from my genius, the work of many years... Ah,' Ned could see his head

33

shaking against the light, 'no, Mr Ludd, that will not and cannot be allowed to happen.'

'What are you doing to my men, you monster?' shouted Ned. 'Why are taking our work and our living by your damned machines. You have no right!'

'My right, dear fellow,' Ludwig chuckled, 'is by right of conquest, or should I say by right of invention. And you, dear Mr Ludd will help me achieve it. Here!' His voice rose in a loud ringing tone. The huge metal figures hissed and stepped in unison to form a ring around Ned, clouds of steam billowing around their metal heads. He grimaced as he saw his men hanging limply in the creatures' arms.

'I see they frighten you,' he chuckled. 'You are right to worry, Mr Ludd.

'Come!' Ludwig pointed at one of the figures. It clanked forward and stopped a mere foot from Ned.

Ned drew back with a gasp.

'No, have a closer look. What do you see?' he commanded.

At first inspection the creature looked like a large man with all the softness of his features turned into hard angles. Dull tin plate outlined the face split only by a small unmoving mouth and two eye sockets. Its head perched neckless on a wide metal body from which extended two metal arms and two metal legs. Directly behind the head was a small aperture where steam trickled out.

'It's hideous!' spat Ned, 'How can you condone such a monstrosity?'

'So you don't like my metal man?' he asked. 'When you consider the power of these creations: they run on steam, perversely using coal mined from your very hills and they are invincible. When I have enough of them I will be unstoppable. Of course,' he put a hand to his short, groomed beard, 'they are only machines. Please, Mr Ludd, take a closer look.'

Ned leant closer and looked into the impassive face. Suddenly he drew away, heart beating rapidly. 'Errgh, what have you done, you inhuman monster!' For he had seen that the eyes of the metal man were not metal but human eyes, wide in terror.'

'Yes, a stroke of genius,' Ludwig said, 'for what is a machine without a driver and what better driver than the human brain?

'Take!'

Ned felt the iron grip of the metal creature immobilise him.

'Now,' Ludwig moved closer, 'I'll achieve two purposes with you and your men: first, new brains for my creations; second, removal of the annoyance you and your followers have been.

'You can be sure, Ned, that while I'll create a place in history no one will even remember you and your Luddites.'

Heart's Desire

'The skill's in the pulling, my boy.' The veined nose dragged my eyes away from his gnarled moving hands. 'All in the pulling,' His eyes disappeared into the creases of his face as he smiled.

I looked back at his hands and what they held.

It wriggled, still warm, still developing. Long, sinuous and shiny, a snake that dove into the powdered colours, taking on hues that made it live as if a pulse of blood moved along its length, beating in time with its maker's heart.

He moved almost too quickly to see; first hands then metal rods then hands again, twisting, coiling, pulling thinner, always moving, a master at his art.

Me? All I wanted to do was taste it, shove it down my throat and eat it in one orgasmic rush.

I briefly scanned his workshop, seeing the never ending array of bottles and their mysterious contents, set on shelves that extended into the darkest corners, feeling the heat from the vast wood-fired ovens, listening with one ear to words, but always my attention returned to the worn wooden table and the life that moved upon it.

Soon the snake of pulled sugar lay to one side, warm, almost pulsing with life while he continued to work his magic. The master fashioned leaves, petals, even thorns, all coloured correctly, all destined for the perfect rose.

My tongue was drooling, instinctively seeking to pick up any lost morsel from the table well before he finished. I didn't hear what he was teaching, so fixated I was on consuming his art.

'There, my boy, what do you think?' he said, proudly showing the roses sitting in the glass tube.

I was struck dumb at how the white sugar had transformed into things of beauty, how the colours grew from within their surface and pulsed at me. They shone with the sweetness of life.

I wanted them.

'You've had an enlightening day,' the master sugarsmith smiled. 'Seeing the transformation of a plain substance with heat and knowledge to become a thing of beauty, of power even.' He nodded to himself, '... of power, yes. The more you work at it the more it transforms and does what the master wants it to do. Easy, yes?'

Seeing the youth agree he continued. 'No. It is not, for you must be aware you are playing with forces you can't understand at your stage, so you treat them with respect, eh? You learn patience, take it slowly, take it carefully, not seek instant gratification or it will come back to hurt you.' He looked carefully at the youth's guileless face and then walked him to the front of the shop. 'So, do you wish to continue, to come back tomorrow?'

Of course I said yes as I walked with the old man, pushing one foot in front of the other, not taking my eyes off my heart's desire until the door closed in my face. I stopped at the window trying to catch a further glimpse but the shop was dark, the roses hidden.

I waited outside, in a darkened recess across the street until night fell and the master sugarsmith had left, locking the front door. I crept back and pushed my nose against the window trying to catch the merest glimmer of colour, until I thought of smashing the glass to get closer.

37

No, I thought, that'd be stupid. There's a back door.

I moved down the alley at the back of the row of shops and found his door. It was solid timber with little sign of age, but the lock was simple. A few hard pushes with my full strength and it snapped open. I was in.

I slipped through the darkened corridor and into the shop. My nose twitched, drawing their scent, enticing me forward. A vague light from the street hit the array of roses, allowing me to see their beauty. I reached out a trembling hand.

'Ouch!' I yelped as a sugar thorn pricked my finger, breaking my entrancement in a moment.

'How dare you,' I growled and snatched at the blooms. A group of blood red petals lay in my hands and I stuffed them into my mouth.

I couldn't stop. In an orgy of feasting I shoved the petals and stems down my throat until I was near to bursting. The sugar filled my stomach and fizzed in my veins. I sat on the table, replete, unable to move.

Sunlight woke me. I heard the turn of a key in the front door and the enormity of what I'd done came home in a rush.

I'll have to get out of here before he finds out, I thought and tried to get off the table. But I couldn't move. I wanted to see who was coming into the shop but my eye was fixed, staring at the ceiling.

I lay there immobile, trying to understand what had happened. I could hear the yells of the master sugarsmith when he saw the destruction I had wrought to his masterpiece. Then movement. I was lifted into the air and had a close-up view of the veined nose and creased face.

'Ah, I had hoped that this time I had chosen my apprentice better.' He held me up to a mirror. When I saw what I had become I tried to look away but I couldn't. The master sugarsmith held a heart-shaped lump of red-coloured sugar, surrounded by lengths of pulled sugar and out of its base shone a single eye. It was looking back at me.

'You just couldn't leave it alone, could you?' I saw him sadly shake his head before I was moved away from the mirror. 'I had hoped, but you ignored my warnings and made your choice. There is nothing I can do.'

I moved through the air, feeling his footsteps vibrated through my blood-red sugar body until I was placed in the shop's window to gaze at the world amongst others of my kind.

Cleansing of the Crypt

'Never thought I'd see the day,' said George Frember, the committee chairman, as he rested on his broom.

'Neither did I, George,' commented Sessila Green, walking past him, a small ripple of muddy water preceding her broom. 'But thanks to us all, it's nearly done.'

'Don't forget about the costs, the draining and now the cleaning. Been expensive for the town.'

George looked at the thin face of Silas Whittaker, the treasurer. 'That should be the end of it, Silas.'

'Nothing'll get done if we stand around talking. This place gives me the creeps.' Gladys Sender, a younger member of the clean-up committee, pushed a strand of blonde hair away from her face. 'I just want to get it finished and then get out.'

'Don't you like the dark?' Tom Greenham winked at Gladys from his darkly handsome face.

'Tom,' she smiled at him. 'There's a time and a place to joke, but in the crypt of the church?'

'Spooky,' Tom laughed. 'They say the old Bishop was buried down here. I wonder how he feels now that the water's gone.'

'Shush!' admonished Reverend Blyth. 'It doesn't do to say things you don't understand.'

'Just wondering, that's all,' said Tom. 'Besides, if the Bishop was buried down here, there'd be a tombstone, or plaque or something, wouldn't there?'

'Haven't seen anything like that,' Gladys commented, her voice thin as she moved into the lamp-lit gloom. 'Anyone else coming?'

The Reverend tugged at his clerical collar, his lined face twisting, 'You young people, you're just too… uh…'

'Irreverent?' asked Tom as he began to follow the slim figure of Gladys disappearing down the far end of the crypt.

The Reverend continued to wrestle with his collar. 'I… uh… didn't mean that. It's just that the Bishop had a… uh… certain reputation.'

'Is anyone going to do some work?' called Sessila. 'We've still got a lot of clearing up. The crypt's larger than it looks.'

They spread out across the vast stone floor, pushing their brooms through the accumulation of many years of silt, gradually moving the muddy water towards the large drain on one side of the poorly lit room. The dark areas caused by the pillars and recesses made the figures appear and disappear, adding to the eerie atmosphere.

'Any chance of a break?' called Tom. 'Just because we're on the cleaning committee doesn't mean we have to work our guts out.'

'Yes,' said the Reverend. 'There's refreshments in the nave.'

Tom waited for Gladys as they headed for the stairs. 'Find any sign of the evil Bishop?' he asked in a ghostly voice.

'No,' she said, rubbing at a streak of mud on her face. 'And don't be so scary. It's bad enough in the dark down there. Cold as charity too.'

'I'm sorry,' he chuckled as she went past. 'I think we need a little warming up. What about I get a radio? Give the old Bishop something to dance to?'

'You never stop, do you? It'd make the Reverend even more nervy,' she said as she climbed the stairs. 'Though it'd keep my mind off being down there.'

'Much more to be done, Reverend?' asked George as they sat on the pews. 'It's hard enough to see what we're doing in the gloom and I'm not as young as I used to be.'

'Take the rest of the day, I'm afraid. And I can't get more lamps – too big an area to properly light up.' His faced twitched. 'I'm keen to get it done too, but couldn't get many volunteers.'

'Except the cleaning committee,' commented Tom. 'And I wouldn't have been on it except... for a sense of civic duty.' He smiled at Gladys.

She blushed and took a sip of her tea.

The music echoed through the vast low-ceilinged crypt, its modern strains out of keeping with the ancient structure.

'What are you doing?' the Reverend hissed. 'It's... it's not appropriate.' He looked around, eyes white in the lamp light.

'Keep your collar on, Reverend. It's to help the living clean the place. Can't disturb the dead, now, can it?' Tom said, giving his broom a large push as he followed the line of Gladys' path.

'Just... just keep it down, if you must.' The Reverend pushed down on his broom as he headed in the opposite direction.

The music overcame the scratching of the brooms as the cleaning committee spread to all parts of the crypt.

'Tom, you following me?' whispered Gladys into his ear.

'Might be,' he answered, putting his hand on her shoulder. 'You know we're all alone down here. Could get lost…'

'Tom!'

'Would you like to get warmer?' His breath was hot in her ear.

'You're not suggesting here, in the crypt? Though, it would be rather… wicked.'

'Are you up for some wickedness, my little witch?' Tom pressed closer.

'Oh,' Gladys gasped as Tom pulled her into a dark, dank recess. 'Ohhh, it's so cold in here.'

'We'll soon warm up,' Tom murmured as he pushed her against a stone ledge.

A faint glow allowed her to see some eroded carving on the nearby wall. Tom felt her shiver. 'I'm not sure…' she whispered as he lifted her onto his folded coat. He silenced her protests with a kiss.

The cold moved around them, deflected by the heat of their lovemaking. Tom grunted and Gladys moaned.

They were unaware of the silent shape rising from the floor behind them.

Tom's fingers tightened on Gladys' shoulders, his face blank, eyes dark holes, neck cording with effort.

Gladys drew in a breath to scream as she watched her lover's face disappear, his features smoothing into the soulless stone shape. 'No!' she cried as she slipped off the ledge.

The man-shaped form confronting her had no face, no features, yet a presence. Cold emanated from it even as she tried to make her feet move. The feel of something ancient trying to infiltrate her body grew as the coldness intensified.

She leant away from the shape filling her vision before the cold stone touched her lips and stilled her protests.

The radio crackled, its music faded. Lamps flickered and died. Silence fell over the crypt. 'What's happening?' the Reverend's voice was high pitched in the dark, 'What's happening!'

'Tom. Gladys. Where are you?' The silence deepened as the deathly cold filled the crypt.

The Craftsman

The craftsman worked the loom, each thread jamming against the other, gnarled hands weaving her tale into the cloth.

She was afraid to look away, unwilling to miss a moment as the magic imbued the material.

Not a word was spoken. He knew what she needed.

She pressed a hand to the dish-like depression in her side, the pain causing her to wince.

'Not long, mistress, before you wear this,' the weaver croaked, eyes on his work. 'Then, when he touches you he'll feel your pain, he'll take your pain.'

'Yes,' she smiled grimly. 'It'll be his death.'

Cassandra

I'm not a fanciful man given to flights of the imagination, nor do I disbelieve the evidence of my own eyes; so the appearance of this apparition in my tent, late on the eve of our crossing into the little travelled wastelands of the Accamad desert, caused me no little anxiety.

I had left my family behind in Stonehaven, an outcrop of a city not far from the Great Steppes of Misomentia. It was there our family had the respect of the trading families in the region and was known for its ability to procure most any spice the known world desired. Thus the hard-gained knowledge of the general location of a rare spice came to the ears of my father. Among its many attributes was the supposed ability to turn back the effects of aging, to give a degree of immortality to the user.

I, in my eagerness to prove that a man of twenty summers could effectively lead a caravan across the lesser travelled regions of Misomentia, asked to be given the chance to find the spice and thus make my name in trading circles.

To my surprise I was granted the opportunity.

That I was entrusted to this role had certain provisos. Hamin, my father's right hand servant and companion, had been foisted on me. Any decision I made had to be vetted by him, but in the end my choice would hold sway: a free man's decision must take precedence over that of an indentured servant. Of course we included the camel drivers and six warriors of a sour and taciturn demeanour, but I was prepared to endure these unlovely travelling companions in order to make my mark.

We had travelled several days due south, taking the option of obtaining fresh supplies from the last village before we entered the beginnings of the desert. Then came our first taste of disquiet.

An old woman, or should I say witch, in mud-coloured clothing with hooded face, was outside the disreputable market as we left. On seeing our direction she began haranguing us, warning us in a sing-song voice about the dangers of the desert. I threw half a copper denarim to keep her quiet but she paid me little heed. Several of my guards exchanged anxious looks as we headed out of the village.

The day we entered the waste lands was hot and dry with winds that grew in intensity as the sun moved overhead. It was a relief to have my tent erected and keep the stinging sand from my eyes, even the heat in that close space was a lesser discomfort. I didn't share my quarters, as befitted my status.

I relaxed after a meal of dried meat and dates, washed down with Stonehaven water. My eyes closed as I lay on the camp bed and listened to the rattle of sand hitting the tent. The heat and closeness of that space faded as I fell asleep.

Cold frosting my nose and cheeks woke me. I took a while to wake as the incongruity of the situation broke through my sleep-befuddled state.

An insubstantial figure stood before me: a young woman dressed in the style of a court: a flowing dress, rich blue with short sleeves exposing well-shaped, bangled arms. Long dark hair framed her pale face

47

dominated by kohl-enhanced eyes; the small pouting mouth and snub nose only contributed to her beauty. I gasped and fell in love.

'Who are you?' I asked inanely.

She smiled prettily, then her brow creased and lips tightened. Her delicate hands rose as if in entreaty, her mouth opened, but not a sound came forth. The rattle of the sand on the tent grew stronger. I raised myself to my elbows, seeking to see more of her and understand her concern.

The woman stepped back, or rather glided to the wall of my tent. My first thought that she was going to leave by the flap but the mere fabric proved no barrier. She began to disappear, colours and form fading.

'Don't!' I cried, jumping up from the bed, but she had gone; just the image of her face, harsher now, imprinted on my mind.

The tent flap pulled aside and the ugly head of Hamin poked through.

'Master Theos,' he asked, 'did you summon me?'

I was not in a state to take umbrage at the intrusion and took time to share my experience.

Hamin listened intently, his face becoming darker as I related my tale.

'Ah Master Theos, I have some news myself that will have bearing on this. I took it as mere gossip until now.'

'Hamin, it's your responsibility to keep me abreast of anything that might affect my mission. My father was most insistent on your role of protector and advisor on this expedition and now I find you have failed in this merest of undertakings.'

I was gratified to see him quail before my remonstration but strove to give him no comfort. 'Well?' I asked, tapping my foot.

48

He bowed his bald head before beginning to speak. I gave him no leave to sit so he shifted from foot to foot as he related the story.

It turned out that the region was rarely travelled. This was due, in part, to the rumour of undying beings roaming the wastelands with a taste for the flesh of man. Such had been legend for centuries, until recently, where a circumstance bought new life to the tale. The lure of riches and, most importantly, the existence of creatures that had fought off death, eternal life in fact, drew a magician and his entourage to venture into the deserts.

This sorcerer, Gaspodian was an egotistical man, so confident in his powers that he took no notice of legend or local warnings before entering the wastelands. Accompanying him was his daughter, Cassandra, rumoured to be as lovely as he was talented.

They disappeared fifty years previously: he, Cassandra and his entire following.

The rumours of riches and a beautiful woman grew, attracting the more foolhardy, but few of those who entered the Accamad desert were seen again. Those who returned spoke little of what they had experienced.

'Hamin,' I scoffed, 'Surely you don't believe that there's much truth to these stories, for if it were so my father would never have risked me on such a venture?'

'So I thought,' he responded, eyes flicking briefly to my face, 'but for the mad witch in the village and now your tale.'

'Hamin,' I laughed, 'you are an old woman yourself. Now leave me.'

He stood for a moment, before giving the merest of bows and slipping away through the tent flap.

To tell the truth the story did unnerve me but my mind was filled with the apparition and my fancies of what I would do with her. The thought of immortality was an extra incentive. I paid no heed to others' misfortunes in the wastelands of Accamad.

The next day started out as any other, hot, dry and a slight breeze that strengthened during the day. We continued due south, initially following a vague track that soon vanished in the sands. The men occasionally spoke amongst themselves and looked anxiously at the bleak surroundings: scrub and sand piled into low dunes that ran east and west along the direction of the prevailing winds. I took little notice, my mind still occupied with Cassandra; for that was what I named my ghost, although I knew the real woman was long dead. At one stage I fancied I saw a large black shape fly across the sun, but when I looked again it was gone.

I was keen to return to my tent that night. The gusting wind drove sand into every crevice of my body. It was maddening and I half hoped that my Cassandra would return.

She appeared, first as a vague shape outlined against the walls of the tent, later as a finely dressed woman of astounding beauty. My mouth dropped open as I drank in her form. She smiled, showing white teeth, lips glistening redly, laughing eyes wide with desire.

I moved trance-like towards her, but for some reason my attraction weakened as I became aware of the unnatural cold. Cassandra frowned, her lovely pale brow creased and she shook her head as if in admonishment of my actions. At that same moment I seemed to wake, hear the rattling of sand on the tent, the murmur of men around the fire. I looked away and when I turned back she had gone.

I fumed, kicked at the sand and knocked over my stool. I even went outside to ask the men what they'd seen, but they only glanced at each other and said little. Hamin drew me aside and asked, most solicitously, what ailed me. On giving a brief account of what had happened he suggested that might best to return home. I was not in a mood to entertain that thought.

Next day was a repeat of those before, hot, dry and the beginnings of a breeze. The men were even more taciturn, if that were possible, despite my orders to go on. So the trek continued; a line of men and camels climbing and descending sand dunes; at least the surface was firm enough to make reasonable pace.

Every now and then my concentration was broken by the flash of black on the very edges of my sight. When I looked back at the men they gave no sign of sharing my experience and the stiffness of Hamin's form just ahead of me didn't encourage me to ask him.

Around noon, we paused for tea. I stood under a temporary awning, mind filled with Cassandra while searching the horizon. Then, at the limits of my vision I saw them. Black shapes as mere specks, rising and falling in the sky to the south. They appeared to be concentrated around a sort of structure but it was too far to tell. I could see that Hamin was looking intently in the same direction.

I called him to me.

'We should head that way,' I said, nodding towards the south. I gave him the opportunity to query my order but he merely shrugged and said the purpose of the expedition was to gain the rare spice and he would obey. I

51

was tempted to ask him what he had seen but left it at that.

It appeared to be a spiral of birds, black and huge, centred on the ruins of an old fortification. I kept my gaze on it as we grew nearer filled with a longing to go to it and see if anything was left under the dark forbidding tower that reached skeletally skywards.

'Hamin,' I called, pointing to the ruins, 'we'll camp here for the night. The ruins will give some protection from these incessant winds.'

'There's still daylight left to travel, Master Theos,' he whined. 'There is something not right about this place.'

'We camp here,' I replied firmly and headed my beast towards the broken-down entrance under the tower.

I was full of bravado at that point and ensured my tent was erected on the sandy floor inside the ruins. I felt no foreboding, just a sense of relief as if somehow I'd arrived home. None of the others shared conversation as they pitched their camp slightly further away where low dunes led away from the fallen stone walls.

Night fell swiftly and, after a quiet meal, I entered my tent already shivering from the sudden cold that can come quickly in the desert. I should have felt lonely so divorced from my men but somehow I was relieved, possibly since I wouldn't have to share Cassandra with them.

I sat on my camp bed and waited expectantly.

She came.

How I loved that woman: her face, her smile, her form tantalisingly framed through the flow of her gown. This time she walked to me, arms upraised, reaching out to cup me with her delicate hands. I stood eagerly, ruthlessly squashing down the thread of unease that threatened our union.

Her fingers slithered over my brow, cold and solid, until they cupped my head between them. Her mouth sought mine.

Full red lips pressed firmly against mine own, sucking my tongue into her mouth. I tasted an indescribable flavour and was lost, having never felt such an overwhelming passion before.

I grew weak, forced to lock my limbs to avoid collapsing. My arms clasped the tiny waist, feeling the tremors of our lovemaking. I never wanted it to end as I put the urgency of my youth into our embrace.

A faintness threatened to overwhelm my senses and I thought to break apart to catch a breath, perhaps move to the bed. But I couldn't move, couldn't break away from her grip and the suction of her mouth.

Suddenly I seemed to shift, to slide up and out of her clasp, to push away and see her before me. I began to panic, for instead of one I saw two forms; Cassandra and that of a well-dressed youth locked together. As I watched the forms blurred, merged into a colour of blue, rich blue. Then Cassandra only remained; her body solid and real. She smiled at me, a satisfied, white-toothed smile and walked out through the flap of the tent.

I reached out to the bed to sit and gain my strength but my grip failed to hold, my hand just slipped off. The numbness of my body spread through to my limbs. I couldn't feel the bed, the ground, anything at all. I fell back and closed my eyes.

The feeling soon left me. I squinted from under an eyelid as daylight filtered through the tent walls. My feet were unsteady when I rose and made my way outside to relieve myself. The white of the desert sands contrasted

53

vividly against the ruins and the dark tents of Hamin and my men.

'Hamin,' I called. 'Attend me!'

No one came, but the sight of the still tethered camels turned suspicion into concern. I quickly determined the tents were empty and found no sign of the men ever having left them.

I spent the day in that damnable place, knowing that my skills were insufficient to find my way back. The camels began calling for water towards evening but I let them suffer, my plight was a great deal worse.

I waited as the sun began to set, casting a ruddy red glow over the dunes. I looked into the darkening sky and could discern huge dark shapes circling the ruined tower in greater numbers than before. I paid them little heed since I had only one thought in mind.

She came walking across the sand, blue and welcoming. I thought to question her, seek word of my men but they had left, maybe for fear of her? As she neared her form closed off any thoughts I might have had. Her lips fastened on mine, the flavour of her infiltrating my being. I didn't want the feeling to end.

I felt my soul drawn to her as we embraced.

In a blinding flash of understanding I realised what I had done, what I had single-mindedly committed myself to for all eternity, her voice reinforcing this decision inside my head.

Your immortality, Theos, has begun.

What Might Have Been

I sail on a ship, I think, for it moves in the rhythmic way water implies, waves catching and tossing a vessel with impunity. Gurgles and sighs softly echo. A faint cry of gulls pierces my cocoon and brings clarity. It is enough to lull my questioning mind and let me drift back to my peace.

Another time, another place the sound reminds. That was when I proudly stood, blonde curls ruffling in the sea breeze, hand resting on the hilt of my newly forged sword given by my liege, the countless craft laden with our war steeds and supplies restless before me. My enthusiasm was boundless, a chance to be in the forefront, the vanguard of the army, to show leadership as befitted the King's son. Oh I was proud, thinking what the ladies of the Court were seeing, a bright handsome man set to lead our armies on a rightful voyage of conquest, seeking to put an end to the depredations of the ruthless Han.

'Oh when can we leave?' My feet itched with impatience as the process of loading our craft continued. So much to prepare, slowly, methodically, carefully. Hard to take by the youth that I was.

'Hold, Jervai.' Grastus, the commander's hand clamped on my armoured shoulder. 'It'll come soon enough. Never be in a rush to go to war.'

I didn't listen; such was my impatience to prove myself to my father and my people.

We sailed that day into a darkening gloom, a blood moon sinking into a red sea, omen upon omen. We thought it augured badly for them, not us. Oh, I wish now that it had.

The voyage blurred, lost in the vagaries of time, only the results left to history, yet even that will be lost.

There were forays into the very heart of the enemy. Men lost, ground gained, victories and defeats. But I digress, for all I cared about was my reputation, how I performed, what reports were sent home. My golden amourered figure at the forefront of the attack, last to withdraw, my bravado on show. For to be a great future king one had to be an heroic leader and I was determined to be such. I ignored the advice of my General, to my cost.

The enemy was running, lines stretched, vulnerable, their courage gone to my eyes. 'There!' I pointed with my gore dripping sword. 'They're panicked, on the run, now's the time to strike.'

'Ware!' warned Gratus, holding his battlesteed with a massive hand. 'The enemy is known for its cunning.'

'Where's your courage, General!' I retorted. 'This is the time to strike, end it all.' In truth I saw it as the moment to stake my claim as my liege's successor, seeing myself on a mound of the enemy astride my white steed, sword pointed to the heavens, seeking approval from my ancestors.

I led a sorte of my youthful fearless cohorts down the hillside in a steaming thunderous roar, weapons thrust forward, certain of a bloody victory. By the time the wiser heads of our army came to join us we were fighting a desperate rearguard action trapped in a cul-de-sac in a deep valley, the enemy too numerous to count.

I'm sure my heroics counted for something as we won the battle and the war. I'm sure of that for I could never have been given the send-off a leader of his people should receive if we'd been defeated, if my body had been lost in the morass of blood, bodies and debris of a beaten army.

At last I heard it, a crackle of flame overcoming the gull cries. I relaxed my mind, preparing for what was to come. Whatever I had done, however I may have won or lost or disappointed, I was receiving a send-off as befitted a warrior of the blood.

And I had to be content with the reputation I left behind as I readied myself to meet my ancestors.

The sound of the flames grew and I almost wished I could feel the heat as the fire consumed my ship and my body.

Antique

'You sure?' I asked my scouter, '20th Century?'

'Yup,' Zilas said without any guile on his face. 'Right on the cusp on moon settlement. Weren't easy to trace, tho.'

'Wouldn't be, would it?' I stroked a hand over my plastique-enhanced face to see if any liquid has oozed out in my excitement. 'Do you have the co-ordinates?'

'Does an ozzle eat lingworms for fastbreak?' I could see a crease crinkling the space between his optics. 'Of course, Chief. First thing I did.'

'It's safe? Untraceable?' I could feel a leg beginning to tremble. It would not do to exhibit too much emotion so I relaxed back into the styroseat.

'As much as I could make it. Took me to areas where you'd never normally venture. Hit my nerves real hard seeing what'd happened to that species, it did.' Zilas snorted a gram of feronin.

I waited while the drug moved through his system, forgiving my underling his habit since the news was so astounding. If it were true I would be able to achieve advancement out of this heavy gravity and into the next echelon of Cranterian society on Zeta B.

'Needed that,' he groaned. 'Sorry, Chief.'

I waved my strength-arm in acknowledgement. 'I understand. I...' A sudden thought crashed between hemispheres. What Zilas had told me didn't make sense. Any genosplice ramseat from that era had been destroyed or subsumed into the matrix. There were none available, whatever the rewards offered. I needed to tread carefully here.

Zilas's loyalty was as complete as any employer could want, but that didn't mean to say that he was incorruptible. I had to make sure.

I used an infallible technique to infiltrate the truth centre of Zilas's upper ganglion. A delicate flick of my pseudo-arm attracted his attention, that and a command phrase had him under in a moment.

I interrogated him with a ruthlessness which appeared to reduce his body mass by half. Eventually I was satisfied no-one knew.

'Uh… uh Chief, w… what happened?'

'A short interrogation, Zilas,' I said firmly. 'Had to be certain. Now replenish your nutrients and we shall deport.'

The trip to Docklands of Old Freeport took little time in the armoured flitter craft. What took time was infiltration into the slums. There was little to remind one of the excitement and industry the area had held almost two hundred years ago, when the prospect of a colony on the Earth's only satellite was promulgated. Rust and plastic was everywhere: wood scavenged decades ago, dwellings broken down and infested by human outcasts and other vermin.

Records have it that our species descended from such a noxious gene pool, before space travel and interspecies breeding cleared out such contaminants. I find that hard to believe, so far have we risen in our journey amongst the stars.

Zilas led me through the mounds of rubble the lowlife called home, tracking unerringly into the depths of the slums. How he had located the existence of a ramseat was beyond me, but my employee did have some hidden talents despite his efforts to destroy himself with the semi-illegal drug, feronin.

I periodically checked my suit's power-pak was at full charge and engaged with my weapon's system. Zilas suddenly stopped outside a low building, reminiscent of 20th Century dwellings. What took my notice was the relative soundness of the house with little of it vandalised, unlike all the others in the vicinity which should have raised my suspicions immediately. But I was preoccupied with being so close to this ancient treasure that I ignored the voice of reason.

'Do ya want to go first?' queried Zilas as he hovered at the solid door, effectively sealing the interior from the filth in the house's locale.

Ignoring the hammerings of doubt in my mind, I lifted my strength-arm from the suit's fire control and pushed. The door showed some resistance before it juddered open. The light was sufficient to see the way was clear: no rubbish on the floor; no vermin within.

'Hold up, outside!' I ordered as I put my sensors to full alert. The presence of my underling in the dwelling could prove fatal to him should he inadvertently trigger my proximity warning.

The first room was clear, showing no reason why the locals had failed to occupy it, although the ambient temperature was unusually low. My misgivings grew.

A flicker of movement attracted my attention. A doorway beckoned.

My strength-arm dropped to the fire control as I moved in that direction. A vague pulsation of light brightened the gloom, like something moving past a window. I reached the opening and peered inside, weapons armed and ready.

60

The window, sound and curtained, attracted my optics. 'Impossible,' I muttered. That there would be unbroken glass and unblemished material was beyond belief.

Then I saw it, against an aged wall, looking firm and in ideal condition for transportation. It seemed that connection to power would be all that was needed to operate the genosplice ramseat. My heart leapt, mind blanking off all the suspicions I should be considering: how did Zilas find the ramseat; why was it in pristine condition; why was the house unspoiled?

A waft of freezing air brushed across my visor, momentarily frosting it. I shivered as my tempcon boosted in response.

I triggered my com-pac to have Zilas ready the flitter, but there was no reply from my incompetent underling.

Repeated sends drew the same result.

'Damn scouter!' I swore as I turned back to fetch him.

Crystals of ice suddenly overcame the heating, making it hard to see the doorway. I paused, waiting for the tempcon to do its job. For the moment I could see nothing yet a flicker of light and dark continued to irritate my optics.

I swung back. The ramseat sat there as before. No change. Yet the temperature continued to plunge.

I thought the shadow over the ancient geneosplice device was another trick of the light until it dawned on me. I had seen all the ancient vids once I knew my posting and recognised the species. Impossibly there was a young female human floating near the ceiling, hair hanging in a sheet in front of her face, slack arms and legs pointing floorwards.

By this time the pressure was affecting me. Gone was my need for the valuable antique and a rise in my status in the Cranterian society. My primary occupation became survival.

I activated the emergency response of my suit that would blast me away to a different locale.

But it failed.

The initial burst of power was sucked away in an instant, all indicator lights fading to darkness.

Ah hell, I thought, I'll just have to get outside and hope I don't need my suit's defences.

Then the real hell happened. The fastenings in my suit gave way and, with a slither, the suit just folded up around my locomotive region. I was exposed and vulnerable in a hostile and unforgiving environment. The air tasted foul when I was forced to take a long, gasping breath. I raised my head as I did so and immediately wished I hadn't.

A face, eyes large in pallid skin was directly in front of me, mouth open in a silent scream.

The girl had come down from the ceiling to meet me.

I was as frozen as the air around me. Her face touched mine and the coldness descended into my mind, and at that instant I knew.

I was betrayed!

The very stuff that remained in my makeup from this ancient world, which enlightened people had attempted to remove from the gene pool made me susceptible to this manifestation of the ramseat – this violator of the very species that had reached the stars.

All around me were revealed disembodied fragments of people who had entered this room and been subsumed by this device.

My brain's synapses gradually failed. I even lost the ability to scream as I became one of them.

Baby's Need

Oswald's jacket was green, if you saw it in a particular light. Spring made it glow, drawing in the power of life until it bulged with purpose. All manner of things were attracted to it.

He had attitude, did Oswald. If you could imagine a hideous old man exposing ugliness that should be hidden from the world, or a maiden fresh in the bloom of youth flaunting her beauty, then you would see his approach to things.

His head projected like an unopened mushroom above his shoulders, several strands of hair pasted across the bald skull. His eyes were a watery blue as if the colour had leached away, face unassuming, small mouth with full lips. No picture, but the jacket seemed to bring him together, gave him a competent air.

When the wind howled, driving sleet and debris through the streets, Oswald could be seen, a brown indistinct figure seemingly shepherding scattered skeletal things before him. Everything was cold and gloomy with the storms of winter. The seasons coloured the jacket.

And he was noticed by the townspeople, for Oswald attracted people. His meandering travels took him across the paths of many folk. Women in particular found his company pleasing although they remembered little once he'd left. Men's suspicions quickly faded when they met up with him. But animals gave him a wide berth, so it was all the more strange when a pet, or companion of sorts, appeared.

After a particularly severe storm, a skitter of elements dogged the man, a ball of leaves and twigs of knee height, holding onto his jacket tails like a baby. Anyone seeing him had difficultly recalling its exact shape.

Lucy had a fascination for the man. She first saw him from her window as the leaf tips were emerging, tinting the trees with green diamonds. Light from the jacket reflected emerald to her eyes and pulled her in. As time progressed she spied on him whenever the fancy took her. It was this fascination that allowed her to notice the jacket morphing with time. It dragged at her, as it absorbed the colours of the world waxing and waning with the rhythm of life. Lucy, on the cusp of womanhood, was irretrievably seduced.

Oswald always appeared not to notice who was trailing him. His watery eyes stayed firmly focused on his path, head erect, shoulders straight and the elemental ball following. Lucy followed too.

Those used to seeing the man wandering through the streets at all hours didn't notice the change when it began to happen. Oswald's head had slowly withdrawn into the jacket, shoulders drooped, body shrunk as if reflecting the season. An astute observer would see the ball more clearly, larger with a defined form as if its elements had coalesced.

The transition, when it came, was swift. It was as if the jacket was taking all that remained of the man. Gone was Oswald's purposeful air, his power that made people step aside, his meanderings now haphazard.

Winter had come, harsh and cold. Oswald walked until the buds began to appear, but as a lesser shadow of a man he had been. His companions followed.

One day, in a blowing gale he stopped, turned and confronted Lucy.

'You following me?' His voice rasped like a rustle of desiccated leaves. The ball murmured in support.

'I... I,' Lucy paused as she peered at Oswald's face. The eyes appeared large and luminous in a creased pallid face, the turn-ups of the jacket framing a shriveled head, the small mouth had lost its plump lips. 'I think I wanted to be with you but...'

All at once a shrill sound emanated from the large ball at his side. She could see that it appeared to be linked to him, vaguely pulsing. Its covering was of skeletonized leaves haphazardly pasted together. She clasped her ears as the sound rose into a scream.

'Baby. Quiet!' hissed Oswald. The howling of the wind became the only noise.

Lucy cautiously lifted first one then the other hand, looking from the man to the ball he called Baby.

'You want to be with this?' His arm swept across the ball, knocking off a few shreds of leaf matter which were whipped away by the wind. Oswald's eyes held hers.

'Uh... no, but.'

His voice rustled. 'You need to know you're making a commitment.'

He was close enough for Lucy to smell his breath, an odour of leafy decay. Her feet refused to move as his eyes filled her vision. She turned her head. He whispered into her ear. She never recalled what he said only what it promised: life in tune with the seasons, with the times, spread so thin yet always there, always able to feel your own presence and your own worth.

She trembled as she felt his skeletal arms on her, her mind flowing into what he was offering. At the last, a small spark triggered a memory of her life.

'No, Oswald.' She pushed him away, pulled her gaze from his and folded her arms under her breasts.

The Baby whimpered.

He assessed her as she stood there, shaking. She wanted to run but his attraction was still strong; she wanted to say *Yes, Oswald*.

'So,' his voice filled her mind, 'you do want to?'

Lucy nodded.

Baby's whimpering grew louder, coalescing into a scream. 'Then you must put your hand in my pocket.'

Lucy heard Oswald's directions clearly over the screaming and moved forward, reaching a hand towards the jacket as if in a dream.

'Now!'

With the word she plunged her hand into Oswald's jacket pocket and next moment she was rubbing her hand furiously on her dress and screaming almost as loud as the Baby.

The pain withdrew, leaving her fingers numb. She held her hand up and inspected it through teary eyes. They were still there, all five digits, but they had a glow about them. She looked across at Oswald. A small smile created a patchwork of lines across his hollow face.

Then she realized. There was no screaming competing with the howling wind. Lucy glanced down towards where the Baby had stood.

'The Baby, it's gone?'

'Come,' he held out a shaky arm almost lost in the jacket's voluminous sleeve. She moved under it. 'I think…' his voice whispered, becoming more indistinct, 'the Baby's needs have been… met, don't you?'

He rested a spidery hand on her rounded belly as the jacket collapsed over her.

The memory of Lucy's life was lost as she adjusted to the jacket's snug fit. She never felt Oswald disappear, his presence vanish. She focused on the feeling of life. The wind died away. She began to walk through the streets in a purposeful way.

The sun came out, highlighting the leafy covering on the trees. The jacket glowed green as the Baby's scream echoed, but only on the inside.

Blood Magic

Her face was lined, eyes closed, body desiccated, limbs bony lengths, colours greys and browns; a pool of red spread beneath her body across the wooden floor.

A beam of morning sun filtering through a gap in closed blinds of the room lit her face.

Her eyelids snapped open. A hiss came through clenched teeth as her white-knuckled hands tightened on the steel that pierced her chest. Her body twisted, legs bent as she silently worked at the stake, wriggling it in minute movements. Each movement drew a stab of pain; each movement added to the flow of blood.

The sound of a foot moving made her freeze and strain to see in the dim room. *'He knows I'm alive,'* she thought. Her hands fell from the metal and words quietly escaped her lips:

By my blood you will sleep... your magic will be worthless.

You will not succeed... not retain your powers.

By my blood... by my blood.

Her head rolled in her efforts, eyes locking on the forms of her coven sisters spaced around her, similarly transfixed to the floor.

'I. Can. Live!' she hissed through gritted teeth.

The agony came in waves. Her eyes closed and head dropped, shallow breaths slowing.

The room grew quiet.

Almost of their own accord her hands inched to the steel pinning her to the boards, working at it, body stiffening in pain.

He had wormed his way into their group. None had disputed him as he was assured and knowledgeable in the dark arts. So the witches of the village of Bablock Hyte had accepted him as the seventh member of their coven, each eager to test the boundaries of their power with the number to complete the magic circle.

The ley line beneath an abandoned house was chosen; 'Better to access the powers,' he instructed. So they followed him. A circle was drawn, encompassing a heptagonal star. They were to stand within it, each at the point of the seven-sided star, at midnight on the changing of the seasons, at summer solstice. Then power would accrue to each of them. More power than they'd ever known.

And they believed him.

She remembered their excitement as the time approached. Never had the witches been able to access such power as he promised. Never in their fumblings with magic had an opportunity been available and they had grabbed it with both hands.

They entered the room in a hush, the atmosphere heavy and expectant. Any noise seemed dulled and absorbed instantly.

He was wearing a black robe, face stern, eyes dark, he had drawn forth a crystal decanter filled with thick liquid and seven small glasses. 'To prepare,' he said. 'To better access the powers.'

And they had believed him.

The liquid left burning trails down their throats.

Then silence, until she awoke to a horrendous pain in her chest and the feeling of life blood leaving her body.

Her sister witches lay around her, steel stakes pinning them to the floor. She fancied she could see glowing astral lines linking them, leading to where he stood at the pinnacle of the star. His arms were spread wide, his face stretched, looking up as he absorbed their life force.

Her head fell back as she realised what he had done. They had been willing victims in his quest for power. They were his power.

But blood gives magic and hope. She set a small, insignificant magic into her flow, the spell of sleep which most witches know.

She lost consciousness.

She had woken and, with renewed effort, kept working at the shaft that pinned her to the floor. She finally broke it free of the wood and slowly rolled over onto her knees. A hand placed in her own red blood was held out, she got to her feet holding the steel that still pierced her chest.

Infinitesimal steps left tracks of blood as she edged her way towards the sleeping wizard, form flushed with power.

She tottered forward, biting her lips to keep from crying out with the pain.

His eyes opened.

Without thought she wrenched the steel from her body and fell forward onto him, the shaft penetrating his chest. He cried in agony as his power flew into her, filling her body with magic, plumping her form, bringing her life.

She watched the man's face change, his expression of horror as he felt his life fading away.

It was good.

Her fingertips sparked, energy filling every part of her. She felt like dancing on the ceiling, letting her magic have expression.

'So this is what he was after. This was why he sacrificed us.'

Her thoughts turned to her five sisters. Could she help them? Could she bring them back to life?

She stood for a moment looking at the still bodies. A smile darkened her face as she stepped away to explore her new power.

Bucket of Salvation

Raith squinted through the filters covering his eyes and the narrow viewports. The sweat prickling his forehead was more from imagination than actual heat but it didn't lessen the primal fear that shook his body.

He scanned the instruments, all screaming at him from the red zone. The guidon threatened to slip under his sweaty palm but he allowed it to edge the pointer in a smooth arc over his flight path. Sure he didn't need it but he had to have some control, had to feel technology didn't take all the decisions. The guidon, his one link to the archaic technology of the 21st Century, allowed him that control, but it didn't still his fear.

A squeal started, heralding a vibration caused by gravitation exerting its iron grip on the ship's structure. Raith knew what was happening: the smooth surface of the ship rippling in reaction to the immense forces it was encountering, while keeping its vulnerable human cargo safe.

Soon, he thought, soon.

A rumble penetrated; familiar, but adding to his paranoia. 'Bloody K-H effect already,' he muttered, thinking briefly of those now long-dead scientists, Kelvin and Helmholtz who gave their name to the solar winds and the reason he was here.

Raith saw the temperature display showing a balmy 30 degrees inside despite the state-of-the-art insulation, yet a mere 4000 degrees C outside. He chanced a look through the slit of the viewport. The flickering flames of the corona were already licking the ship, ready to toast this intruder as the temperatures rose. The interior of the ship seemed alive with flames coruscating in colours from golden through red to the hottest of white.

He concentrated on the plotted elliptical path, knowing the moment of release had to be precisely timed, for the super-strengthened platalloy would not take more than a moment or two to melt away in temperatures of the targeted coronal hole emitting the fast solar wind from the polar region of the sun.

His hand hovered over the button, relying on feel rather than computerised timing. Even the most advanced software failed to take in that extra element: the element of knowing precisely when the magnetic snare could be engaged. The factors affecting a successful snatch of 'star stuff', the molten plasma of the sun, could vary as easily as an unexpected flare or a variation of patterns within the solar wind. The human mind added just the extra factor which could mean the success or failure of the mission.

Now, his mind screamed, *now.*

His hand plunged down and the powerful engines fired the pulse deep into the coronal hole whose vortex drew a continuous stream of plasma from the surface, over a million kilometres below.

The ship shuddered, taking the strain as the magnetic field captured a 'bucket' of plasma and attempted to heave it from its source. Raith grimaced as he thought a fisherman striking and reeling in his catch, but the stakes were much higher here. If he lost, he would pay the ultimate price.

The instruments showed that the capture had been successful and the ship's engines immediately went to full power. The g-forces were exceptional despite the stasis field and Raith pulled with the ship, muscles straining, joints cracking. This was the moment. Would the power and planned trajectory enable them to break free with their cargo or would they be absorbed into the gigantic maelstrom below?

All monitors were flashing warning signs and indicators had moved beyond the red zone. The fight was at a standstill.

Raith's gaze flashed around the cabin, briefly noticing the temperature standing at 35 degrees C while waiting for the inevitable slide back into the sun. He had one card to play, employing the comparatively minute power of the positional thrusters, normally only used in docking.

His hand snapped up to the panel and flicked the switch.

The temperature climbed. 40 degrees. He didn't look at the outside temperatures.

He felt a slight give amongst the shuddering and flexing of the ship. Pressure started dropping, temperature rising.

Sweat sheened his eyeballs as he hazily registered the beginnings of a forward motion along the prescribed path whose trajectory slowly swung away from the sun.

He had no choice now. The mission had to succeed on its own. The human element could not survive with the increasing heat.

Raith took a final look through the viewport, closed his eyes and initiated the final sequence.

The dark cool didn't register at first. Sweat poured out of him, suit wringing wet: the babble of voices, a cold compress on his forehead and sweet fluid trickling down his throat.

'Unlimited power.' 'Plasma.' 'Sun.' Words trickled into his mind. Grinning faces above came slowly into focus. He felt the pats on his shoulder, his hand being shaken.

He had succeeded. The colony would now have the power it needed to survive. And his etheraform had successfully returned to his body. It had been worth the years of planning and the technology that had been created, enabling the mission to give hope for the future.

Raith felt an overwhelming satisfaction that his unique gift had allowed this to happen yet sad he wouldn't live to see the future he had created.

The change in his etheraform became more noticeable, its substance thinning at the very moment of triumph. He fought briefly and then let it happen. It would be some moments before joyous people around him would notice he had gone, absorbed by what he had created.

Ship of the Gods

Harsh lights hit my eye, cascading in a multitude of glittering colours to drive a sick feeling deep in the pit of my stomach. Impassive gilt-covered features gazed stony-eyed across the vast space, adding their presence to the sense of wrongness in the room.

I continued through the cruise liner's Egyptian-themed dining room despite the prickling of my skin focusing instead on the royal blue carpet as we were led to our booth by the smiling wait staff.

'Your seats, Madam. Sir.'

We slid across red and gold satin fabric to settle facing each other over white tablecloth and silver cutlery. A fan of glass with its etchings of Egyptian hieroglyphs silhouetted my wife, a stylised jackal peering over her shoulder.

I shivered until distracted by the proffered menu.

'I'm liking the seafood,' she said, tapping the page.

'Steak for me.' I dropped the menu and gazed around the vast room. Wait staff scurried, guests sat, noise burbled while a vast presence overrode it all.

'Would you like a drink, Sir?' The beverage waiter interrupted.

'Uh, Glennfiddich. Double. On the rocks.'

He scurried away.

I wriggled my shoulders, trying to relieve an increasing ache.

'Oh look, a Sphinx.' Joan pointed over my head.

I slowly twisted, taking in the large, winged figure, lion body, human face suspended in the glass behind my

77

head. Enigmatic eyes looked into mine. I saw starlight in its gaze.

'Your drink, Sir.' The clunk of the glass on the table drew my attention.

The steak was good but the whisky was better. During the meal I relaxed, leaning back until my head touched the glass. A feeling of lassitude crept through me. Joan's voice and the frenetic surroundings slowly faded. It was cold, so cold.

'Mark. Mark!'

My eyes snapped open. 'What?'

'We have to go!' she hissed. 'You're falling asleep. It's embarrassing.'

I slowly got to my feet and followed her stiff back out of the dining room, feeling a sense of loss.

We settled into our seats to watch the 'Fun at Sea' show and I closed my eyes, attempting to ignore the bright blue eyes of Horus observing me from high on the walls. Instead, I wallowed in the strangeness of the dining room while the entertainment continued. Joan refused to talk to me.

Next mealtime it was back to our allocated booth. 'Don't embarrass me again or it's the last cruise we'll go on,' Joan warned.

I looked to the Jackal behind her, felt the Sphinx at my back before nodding. I didn't want to repeat what had happened the previous night.

We sat with the creatures at our back. 'Keep them coming,' I told the beverage waiter.

Joan's voice droned, the food was tasteless while I explored another world.

I felt myself drawn to the glass panel until my head rested against the Sphinx's giant paws.

A pain drove into my arm.

'Mark, what's the matter? What are you doing?'

I pulled back from snapping at my wife. 'Nothing. Let's go. Not hungry.'

Cutlery fell to the ground as I stood abruptly and led Joan from the dining room. I didn't, couldn't look back.

The grey ocean echoed my mood, the waves chopping haphazardly, trying for direction and failing. I hung over the railing of the great ocean liner, feeling myself slipping into the formless water beneath me. The pull was great. Joan had retreated to our cabin while I tried to cling to my sanity.

Despite her questioning I couldn't tell her what was happening. I didn't know myself.

That night the eye descended, blue and strong, peering into my brain while I slept.

The crunch of sand from strong legs pacing across the desert, flying under Ra's pitiless gaze, Horus's messenger wearing my magnificent body, lungs drawing in gulps of air as I flew from what lurked behind me.

The Sphinx drew the Eye away, letting in black shapes. I fought to understand them, give them form. And through it all the Jackal laughed.

The ship moved on, countless fathoms beneath it, miles to go before our next destination. I was carried along, a mere mote in the vastness.

I woke to an empty bed as the cabin door slammed. I knew I had to fight, had to do something to stop whatever was happening.

The liner's library contained several references to Egyptology, allowing me to investigate my unusual experiences. While the characters I'd seen were benign except for Anubis, the jackal-headed god, the representation appearing behind the head of my wife. Horus and his messenger, the Sphinx were there to protect, defend even. So why did I feel so disassociated from Joan and reality? Why did I feel an affinity with the Sphinx?

I needed to solve this, to mend things with my wife. I needed to return to the dining room with her even though I didn't want to go back.

The God of the Dead watched me as I shuffled past into my seat. He seemed to envelop Joan as she sat in front of him. Even my companion, the Sphinx seemed to avoid my look. I sat in front of it and immediately leant back into its presence. The usual whisky was placed in front of me without my asking. I gulped it down while Joan meticulously studied the menu. The waiter went for a refill while I felt some relief at the weight of the Sphinx's paws on my shoulders. The Jackal waited.

Our next port was two nights away. Two nights before I could leave, take Joan away from the Ship of the Gods, but I had to sleep.

The Sphinx's visage shifted, changed shape, ears elongating, eyes dark and penetrating, laughter echoed. I couldn't run or hide. It grabbed me by the scruff of the neck and began to lead me down into the dark. I resisted, my paws struggling against the desert sand but the God was strong with the weight of a hundred thousand deaths behind it. I snarled, wings flapping at the increasing pull on my soul.

Darkness surrounded me; just a circle of light far above. Then I noticed a slowing of my descent as the light far above turned blue. The Sphinx's roars grew joyful. The God of Protection had answered his servant's call and put its might against the God of the Dead. Slowly the pull changed and I felt myself rising towards the light and the blue eye of Horus.

A howl of rage echoed as I sat up in my bed.

'Not again!' Joan shouted.

'Please. A bad dream,' I gasped, reaching for her. 'Just bad dream.'

The experience had shaken me badly but fortunately my wife had some compassion and agreed to come to dinner with me that night.

I suddenly realised we were being led to a different area of the vast dining room.

'What?' I said, looking back. 'Why aren't we going to our normal seat?'

'Sorry, Sir, we're sitting you elsewhere tonight. Unfortunately there was an accident – a glass panel broken.'

I pulled away and strode towards our old booth. My jaw dropped and I reached blindly for Joan's hand. The Jackal was disfigured, a jagged crack driving through its engraved face.

Out of the corner of my eye I saw the engraved Sphinx from my side of the booth. It had an enigmatic smile; its eyes blue.

I was relieved to feel Joan return my grip.

Deadly Picture

The body lay hunched in a foetal position against an unremarkable, brown-coloured wall deep within the ruins of the ancient city. The archaeologists puzzled over the position of the body, what had caused his death and led to him to lie there for millennia.

The newly discovered ruins hadn't been thoroughly explored and were providing intriguing clues to a tragedy that had cut down the civilization in its prime.

An excited archaeologist noticed the dust-covered wall had a fascinating incompleteness. 'Dig near the base,' he ordered.

The spade of a worker dug deep into the sandy soil. He lifted his spade for a second push into the soil when a cry stopped him.

All eyes rose to the wall. A section had shifted, dust falling, revealing portions of a picture coloured like the clay that had formed it. They watched as dust fell in clouds changing the scene, like sun falling across the water.

A picture grew. Brown forms: people, animals, plants and an ancient city landscape. Then, more astonishingly, colour flooded the scene, like a switch turned on. Cold clay turned to light. Vibrancy added life. Movement began.

The onlookers were spellbound. Never had they seen anything like it. The picture before them wasn't old, wasn't static. It was life, living and real, like a voyeuristic view into a world that had existed, there in front of them. They fully expected sound to complete the picture, but all was acted out in silence.

A group of women talking while washing clothes in the fountain, children running past with shrill screams, excited dogs barking, a donkey braying, two old men muttering over a game board, several soldiers marching by, hobnail boots clattering on cobbles.

Soundless.

Suddenly all activity stopped, heads turned. Something, unheard by the observers, had attracted them.

The scene darkened, a pall overcoming the light. Huge clouds of dark billowing ash grew in front of astonished eyes, rolling and roiling with flickering red and yellow embers held aloft. Palm trees bent, dust flew, people and animals panicked, every activity forgotten. Silent screams as the clouds blotted everything out.

Colour leached away, returning to clay-coloured walls.

Spades fell from nerveless fingers, the archaeologists rushing for the entrance, pushing for the light.

The expedition fled from the ember-filled dark cloud rolling over the ruins of the ancient city. And, like the warning of the long dead inhabitants entombed in the valley, it was soundless.

A Debt Called In

I tightened my grey overcoat as I ran through the busy city streets in the chill morning, sirens already echoing behind me. A weight, hot and hard, pulled at the inside pocket of my coat. I supported it with my hand.

The noise, I thought, that's what did it.

The sound they'd made, a kind of muted popping was hardly discernible from the traffic noise of the city outside. But me? Well, I had to defend myself and it was loud; my gun didn't have a silencer.

I'd spent all night pacing the floor trying to work out how to handle the letter that had been pushed under my door–a thick white envelope of the kind you'd normally expect from a reputable establishment. That, and the contents, gave me the sleepless night. One day was all they'd allowed to come up with money or I'd be losing part of my anatomy. They gave no thought to my circumstances or ability to pay. Just the letter; and the threat.

In the end I resolved to front them, demand they allow me more time to pay. I took my dad's well-oiled old Colt from the war to give me confidence.

My real problem was that I thought they'd be still asleep from a long night of extorting money from their victims, not sitting at the table in a semi-alert state. They were not pleased to see me.

I suppose I made it difficult for them to think otherwise as I'd just kicked in their door and caught them sitting at a table in their kitchen, counting money.

They seemed startled by my entrance.

The older brother, black eyebrows meeting over his sallow face, slowly put down a sheaf of notes and began to stand. The younger one, no picture himself, moved a hand to the pocket of his dressing gown.

'What're you doing?' he growled. 'You could'a knocked.'

As I hunched over, trying to catch a breath to demand they give me more time, it started, the popping. He remained seated, firing through the pocket of his gown. I heard the buzz of the bullets, jumped to the side of the doorway and heaved out my gun.

The older brother had moved to the kitchen bench and held a gun fitted with a bulbous silencer. He too began to fire.

I had no choice and added the crashing roar of my Colt. The men had dropped to the floor, motionless, by the time my gun was empty. I thrust it inside my overcoat and ran.

The sirens grew louder before they began to fade. *Thank God*, I thought, *they can't know where I've gone*.

I ducked between several cars and headed towards a commuter car park. I had a fair cramp at this time, just under my ribs and was panting fit to bust. *Should of kept fit*, I thought as I stumbled along.

I dodged around a tired old horse tethered to a garish carriage at the kerb and stopped. The incongruity of the horse and carriage grabbed me. It wasn't one of those horse and cart tourist attractions that you occasionally see in the evenings trotting the city streets, carrying people with time on their hands and more money than sense. It was completely different.

The horse was your normal brown gelding, standing there comfortably. It had a touch of colouring, blue and red on its harness but not much else. The carriage on the other hand looked like a painted theatre prop. The wheels, suspension and trimmings were a greeny-gold, dull with a metallic shine; the interior was bright red velvet with cushions of the same deep blue of the horse's harness.

I looked around for the owner but he was gone, probably off for a coffee to warm himself up. The people moving along the sidewalk took no notice of me or the horse and carriage.

I jerked as the siren grew louder. *Damn,* I thought, *I'll have to hide somewhere.* At that moment I noticed a glint where the sun reflected off the trimming. The surface appeared to quiver.

I moved closer and pushed at a wheel. My finger dimpled the surface, like a ripple on oily film.

I ignored the urge to flee and edged along the length of the carriage. The delicate lines on the woodwork and cushioning were like a glossy plastic, shiny and reflecting the light. Even the harness was embossed in a shining tracery that shivered as I watched. Conscious of the sounds of pursuit I stepped away and turned to cross the road. That's when I felt the presence behind me.

'Oi!' said a voice, 'you'll be wanting a lift then?'

I swung around and the gun slipped out from under my overcoat. It fell with a clunk. But the man facing me didn't follow my horrified eyes to the ground; he just stood waiting for my answer.

I quickly scanned the area but couldn't locate the weapon on the grey surface.

'Well, do you want to ride or not?'

My head jerked up and I stared at the speaker. He was small like a jockey, but stocky, dressed in red breeches and a blue coat. His eyes, a deep brown watched my face as he waited for an answer.

86

No threat here, I thought as I looked across the street to an alleyway, planning where I'd run. But I was tired. I gazed at the horse and the carriage, now appearing more solid than its surroundings. The horse turned his head as if emphasising his master's request. Its eyes were a deep brown.

I reached out and put my hand on the side of the carriage. It felt solid, reassuring.

'If you decide, then just get inside. I'll be waiting.'

The little man climbed up onto the perch and picked up the reins.

I could hear a second siren join the first and nervously moved to one side. My foot kicked the gun. I began to bend to pick it up but found I couldn't be bothered. If the driver hadn't noticed it maybe I could leave it where it was.

The alley across the wide road beckoned as a dark hole in a blur of buildings, but the sirens were loud and I suddenly felt too tired to run any further. The sound of tyres a short distance away made up my mind. I pulled myself into the carriage with some difficulty. I sat there, still catching my breath, perversely appreciating the softness of the deep blue cushions, I heard the roar of the police cars from behind but didn't dare look round.

I saw the driver's head move slightly then he flicked the reins. The horse moved off at a slow walk, ignoring the braking cars.

I couldn't stand it. I twisted around in the seat. Two police cars blocked the street behind us. I heard another siren ahead so I crouched lower to take advantage of the carriage's limited cover.

The horse increased its pace from a walk to a trot.

When a police car pulled up in front of us, leaving little room for the horse and carriage to get by, I knew I was in trouble.

Then the driver flicked the reins and the horse trotted straight up to the car and squeezed past. The officer didn't even glance our way as he ran on down the street.

I followed his progress. He stopped where his companions were gathered. *They must have found the gun.*

'Shit!' I muttered. 'I knew I should've picked it up.'

'Eh?' The driver had swung around on his seat.

'Ah, I was just worried about the police back there,' I gasped.

'Don't concern yourself,' he said. 'It will be of no matter to you.'

'What?' I said. But the driver had turned back. The horse moved to a fast trot.

I turned back and focused on the knot of police. I could see them as if they were in a spotlight, looking at the ground. An ambulance had joined them and two paramedics were pulling something onto a stretcher. A grey overcoat covered whatever it was.

My throat tightened and lungs hurt as I gasped for breath.

'No! It can't be!' I shouted at them. They didn't seem to hear me. I swung around to the driver but couldn't connect with him. My fingers bit into the upholstered sides.

The streetscape shivered and disappeared. The horse and carriage moved at a gallop into the blackness that seeped into my existence.

I couldn't concentrate after that.

Sting in the Tail

I didn't need to see my reflection to be upset.

Huge bat wings stretched 20 foot either side of my scaly, snake-like body. My head was hideous, spikey ears and other projections outlining a cruel mouth with dagger-like teeth. My clawed feet were tucked up against my body as I flew, while my tail... well my tail hung down, high over me, with its venomous sting poised to strike.

All-in-all a terrifying picture.

Of all the aspects I'd adopted through the long years as a servant-cum-assassin for my Master, Bretnezus, the Jaipur of Arksan, this was the worst. Not that I had a lot of choice. No matter how well I pleased him, how viciously I dispatched his enemies, how efficiently I'd carried out my tasks, he was never satisfied.

Dependent on the vagaries of his humour and who had displeased him, he would choose the form for me to adopt when I went on a mission, the geass he held gave me no choice.

Young, lithe of body, curves in the right places, dark hair curling across my dimple-cheeked face was my favoured aspect, one I believed to be my original form. But Bretnezus determined which form I could use and any show of defiance was punished. Hence Serayer, a creature of passing beauty was as hideous as the Jaipur could make me.

My thoughts dissolved as an eddy snatched my wings, pushing me higher into the evening sky towards the thin grey clouds that hung over the vast barren land. I adjusted the beat and settled into a regular rhythm. It had been so long since I had last flown that my instinct took a while to kick in.

My large reptilian heart gradually slowed and I was able to think about the task ahead and ignore my eons-old gripe with my cruel master.

I was to make a statement for my master. Bretnezus needed to remind the conglomeration of states wrestling for control of the known world, that Arksan was pre-eminent. Far too long his attention had been insular, focussed on settling his own issues, ensuring lines of succession were appropriate, that blood would out.

The existence of a geass-bonded assassin made his decisions easy to enforce and so had he done, with extreme ruthlessness.

Me? I had a modicum of qualms as I stole the heart of a young prince, literally, or sucked the blood of a fractious teenager seeking to avoid the ordained rule – the wizened husk left where it would best remind the populace the price of rebellion.

Now Bretnezus, satisfied matters at home were secure, had refocused on the world around him and set his sights on the newly-crowned Jaipur of Samarkand. The Jaipur had died, supposedly of old age, allowing the accession of his son, a man with little respect for the old ways: such traditions as fealty to the Jaipur of Arksan.

Soon the barren plains gave way to the muddy brown of the city of Samarkand. Thin smoke trails of dung fires rose into the sky, adding their pollution to the pall that marked the city. It spread like a freshly-made turd on the harsh land that even now was lightening as tendrils of the rising sun crept through the thin clouds.

Dawn, I thought. Time to pay my respects to the young usurper and remind him of his responsibilities. I flapped through the gloom and took no notice of the odd scavenging buzzard startled by my presence, nor the yapping of dogs in endless bravado until I neared. My goal was my focus and nothing would distract me.

The minaret topping the palace resembled a skull and the dark eye socket openings made a fair place to land. My claws snagged the wooden railings, bending under my weight until I hit the tiled floor with a clatter. I glanced around, tail poised, sting ready, but the room situated under the tiled roof was empty. I swung to face the anticipated horde of guards issuing forth from the dark stairwell. I was greeted by silence.

I paused, shook my teeth-filled head and headed for the stairs, claws scraping the tiles.

It was here it happened. An unfortunate transition from my armoured fighting form to my favoured aspect. Why my master chose to make me so vulnerable at the time of my entry into his enemy's home was perplexing.

So it was that I, a woman of surpassing beauty, was exposed. I snagged a light curtain from the window and draped it around my naked form as cover. My mind settled into assassin mode and, despite my lack of teeth and poison, I resolved to make best use of the body I was in.

I padded on bare feet down a set of steps that descended the minaret's tower, my nose unerringly tracking the young Jaipur's odour. I pushed a lock of dark hair behind my ear, adjusted my translucent drape to clearly reveal the thrust of my breasts, set my mouth in a winning smile and pushed open the bedroom door.

What did I expect to see? What was waiting for me? I anticipated a wall of guards surrounding a pimpled, fat-bellied youth who realised his time had come. They would hesitate when they saw Serayer of the comely aspect and in that moment I'd strike, leaving a drained husk as a reminder before returning to my master.

Or so I thought.

A light breeze ruffled the finest silks that surrounded a large bed, yet no-one was in sight. My assassin's nose twitched. He was there.

Magic. I felt it as a tickle of breeze along my sensitive skin, a lifting of hair at the nape of my neck, cold fingers pulling away my temporary covering. I spun on my heels, hands clawed but there was no-one.

A press of soft lips on my bare shoulder startled me and I swung my arm in a vicious blow, connecting with nothing; a caress along my flank made me tense. My muscles clenched, ready to drive fingers through eye sockets, then a tweak of my breast came from nowhere.

And so it continued. The moment I paused, something else assaulted my person until I was left sweat-sodden and distraught. Nothing like this had ever happened to me in my many years of service. Never had I experienced such helplessness.

I backed into a corner and tried my utmost to return to the form I'd arrived in but nothing obeyed my will. I remained, naked and vulnerable, at the mercy of whatever assailed me. My heart, my human heart, shook my body with its rapid beats as I scanned the room. I tensed, cursing until the air thickened in the centre of the room.

A tall, muscled form appeared, long black hair surrounding a clean visaged face, steely gaze fastened on me. He smiled, a sardonic tilt to an eyebrow.

'Welcome, Mistress Serayer,' his voice rumbled.

'You... you!' I spat. 'What are you doing to me?' I struggled to rise.

'I?' he smiled, his dark eyes assessing me. 'I am doing nothing, yet you, my beautifully formed intruder, are in my home?'

My mind tried to cope with the implications of my situation. Standing in front of me, in full control was my target, Erasimus, the Jaipur of Samarkand.

'Does the aged Jaipur of Arksan wish to pay his respects to my new position, or is he seeking something more permanent to remind me of his need to have Samarkand subservient to him?' Erasimus cocked his head to one side.

I meanwhile shuffled closer to him, seeking to appear innocuous yet still trying to carry out my mission.

'Serayer?' A corner of his smile lifting.

I looked at him out of long-lashed eyes, while digging my nails into my clenched palms.

'I think you and I need to talk.'

'Uh huh,' I edged closer, a light sheen of sweat covering my body. I was within striking distance yet all I could do was strain against invisible bonds.

He took a step forward, his face no more than a hand span from mine and looked at me from dark eyes that seemed bottomless; and those lips, firm and kissable.

Why was this happening? This was the man I was sent to kill, within reach but I couldn't carry out my task; I was thinking with my body rather than my head.

He moved closer.

Sometime later I lifted my head from a muscular chest and gazed in befuddlement around me. I was lying sprawled across Erasimus in a naked, sweat-soaked tangle on the large soft bed.

I struggled to understand my situation when I felt the pull of my master's geass on me. My hand rose, fingers

93

extended as I readied myself to drive them into the vulnerable neck of my victim. Then his eyes opened and he pulled me to him.

My body responded and I forgot my mission, again.

I stretched luxuriously and turned to watch the man beside me get to his feet and slowly dress. He smiled and gestured to a recess in a wall.

'Please find something to wear in there, Serayer.' Erasimus's eyes passed over me and I felt a familiar tingle of response. 'Then we will eat while we determine what to do about you.'

I managed a quick wash down from a basin before dressing in loose green silk trousers and a matching top cut to reveal my midriff. During that time a table covered with fruits and cheeses had been set up. Erasimus indicated I should sit and eat my fill.

The pull of Bretnezus's geass came in various strengths as I walked warily to the table, yet it never was strong enough to cause me to attack my lover. I ceased worrying as I accepted the strong mint tea from Erasimus's hand. Time enough for that, I thought.

'So, my lovely assassin,' he said when we had finished eating. 'What do you think we should do?'

At that moment the pull to carry out my master's task was overwhelming, driving all pleasurable thoughts from my head. The need to change to my armoured form brought an automatic reaction and I could see my human hand striving to alter.

'Ah!' Erasimus nodded his head, 'For all our connecting I see you haven't changed.'

The geass faded and I slumped back, tears filling my eyes. 'I… I can't help it,' I sobbed, the hardness of my

94

assassin's life sinking deeper within me and a soft feminine side revealing itself.

'It would be nice to be with you without the need to be on my guard, without the use of magic, I admit.' He passed me a soft cloth to wipe away my tears. 'How would we best achieve that?'

I gazed dumbly at his thoughtful face, my emotions and needs at war within me. This was the first time in centuries of servitude I realised someone was after me for myself. If only that could be, I inwardly sighed, but my hard master and my death-filled past could never let that happen.

Erasimus reached over and took my shapely jaw in his hand. 'Your master has a strong hold on you; the geass is most powerful. There is only one way to remove it.'

I blinked as hope filled me. Could this man be going to help me, go against the most powerful sorcerer in the land, for me?

The hope quickly faded. I pulled my head away and walked to the door leading to the stairs before looking back. 'No, my love, that's not possible. I must return and be punished for failing in my task. You cannot know how powerful Bretnezus is. I must go.' I turned and slowly ascended the stairs.

I entered the roof top room and the familiar feeling came over me. My dainty hands and feet curled into clawed appendages, my face became a hideous mask and wings burst from my armoured shoulders, ripping the remnants of my green silk clothing into shreds. I balanced awkwardly on the railing and, wings beating, leapt out in the evening sky.

I had spent the best day of my life with the man I had come to kill and left with no regrets. I doubted Bretnezus

95

would destroy me as he valued my use too highly but my being would be put through much torture before he was satisfied.

I had no regrets as I lifted towards the thin grey clouds that always seemed to cover the land and prepared for the long journey home.

I was dazed and had no awareness of my surroundings or I wouldn't have been caught.

A huge black form in a rush of wind buffeted me, tumbling me downwards before I could react. I snarled and spun around, claws open, stinger raised as the huge shape attacked. The creature's body crashed onto me rendering my stinger useless, holding me, forcing me from the sky until we hit the desert floor in a flurry of dust.

I snapped and struggled furiously until a voice whispered in my ear. 'Calm down. Be still.'

'Erasimus? Is that you?' I relaxed into the embrace of the huge, scaled body.

'I could not let you go,' he said, sharp teeth near my spikey ears. 'You are mine. I'm coming with you.'

'You fool!' I hissed. 'He'll kill you.'

'No,' Erasimus cocked his huge head, 'if you work with me we will overcome Bretnezus. I've a mind to live without the fear of tyrants deciding what I should do.'

'You fool,' I repeated, pushing into his comfortable body.

'Maybe, but it's worth a try,' his voice said smugly in my ear.

I nodded without thinking, hope rising within my breast as we broke apart and leapt into the sky.

Our huge wings pulled us into the night, beat matching beat. I couldn't help eyeing the magnificence of Erasimus next to me, the long neck extending into the huge, scaled body and each thrust of the powerful wings. And then the assassin part of me returned. I noticed a pale gap at the nape of his neck, a vulnerable portion in the skin of the armoured beast.

A drop of poison oozed from the tip of my sting and I drifted closer. Watching. Waiting.,,

Choice

No sounds for months. The moon continued its phases, waxing and waning. The night was crisp and clear. The light glimmered across the ice, making a transient, yet deadly road; one our kind couldn't resist travelling. No-one trod its smoothness. The way lay open. Welcoming, quietly innocent; enticing me, in my emaciated state to follow its path. Time meant nothing now. Its future barren, its past sealing the memories.

Did I take the offer or turn back? Either choice would likely mean my death.

They were determined, minds fixed on their goal. Their bodies were taut and moving in a regular rhythm, eating the miles across the wastes. Bows unstrung but held ready. The moon provided light to reveal the tracks black in the snow. Easy to follow, easy to see weariness in the gait; the taste of the coming kill acrid in their mouths.

Tuplek urged them on. He held the sacred knowledge. He had ordered the cull. It was he, with the shaman's iron blade, who removed the pelts of their kills.

His creased eyes looked at his companions, Akiak and Nuklik, seeking sign of flagging. He grunted as he saw their resolve and urged an extra effort from himself.

So near, he thought. *So near*. He could see the silver fur in his mind's eye and knew they were close. His free hand clenched in his glove, aching to rip the pelt from the final Dire wolf–destroying - the last would give him their power, the spirits of the beasts.

'Move!' he grunted. 'We're close.'

They came through the last of the scattered snow-thick bushes and began the descent to the frozen lake. Tuplek paused, scanning the white wastes lit by the waxing moon. A flickering shape, dark then light caught his attention. His heart skipped a beat and a rush of adrenalin flooded his body. His goal was in sight.

They moved onto the ice.

Drifts of snow were all that kept her from catching sight of her pursuers, but she knew they were there. She followed her line of light, darting between shadows of the drifts cast by the angled moon, instinctively seeking the clearest ice where paw prints were unlikely to show.

Her breath plumed the air from open jaws, head down. Too tired to lift, test the air and see the way, always maintaining her pace, using her last reserves. Her heart jumped, body instinctively skittering sideways from a raven-plumed arrow striking the ice. Her pace quickened.

In desperation she sought the thinnest ice where her pursuers might fear to go. It offered the faintest of hopes. She crouched, moving at speed towards the centre of the lake. The ice creaked. Another black-plumed arrow skimmed her shoulder. Soon she would have to turn and face them.

Even as the thought entered her mind a strong vibration reverberated through her paws. The ice had broken. She swung around, lifting her muzzle in hope. Where there had been three hunters only one remained - the Sharman, the most dangerous.

Taking no time to reflect she forced another effort and loped towards the low silhouette of the distant shore.

99

Tuplek was philosophical about the fate of his companions, their deaths in the lake's icy waters merely incidental to his ultimate goal. He could see the she-wolf was flagging, her end in sight. He would accept her sacrifice. He carefully skirted the fractured ice and followed his prey, arrow ready on his tightly strung bow.

He saw her stagger off the icy surface and into the low bushes that fringed the lake. She was at the limits of her strength; it would be easy to take her life.

He thought of the power he would gain as the Dire wolves' strength entered him. The culmination of a lifetime's planning was nearing fruition, at his hand. But he cautioned himself, he still had to kill the last wolf, for even at the end of her strength she was a dangerous adversary.

No, he thought, I will shoot her from a distance, and take her power as she dies.

He followed her tracks onto the snow-covered land, bow raised.

The light from the low moon contrasted, bright and dark, white and black. Paw prints in the snow led to a clump of stark vegetation. He paused, pulled back the string and slowly approached. His instinct told him she had not gone on, that she was waiting within the sparse cover ready to confront him. Tuplek needed a sight of the beast, a clear shot to its heart. He steadied, stilling his breathing, waiting for it to reveal itself.

A sudden upwelling of snow from the centre of the bushes made him almost release his arrow, but he squashed the impulse. He thought he could see the silver of its fur but he paused uncertain.

100

The wolf appeared to stand on its hind legs, twisting even as he thought to release his arrow. Its body elongated, stretching taller, higher than he thought possible. The silver fur seemed to dissipate revealing skin, white in the moonlight.

The new form turned to him, high breasts, long legs and arms of exquisite beauty, silver hair cascading from her head across her shoulders. She smiled and stepped out of the bushes.

Tuplek stood entranced, mouth open, arrow falling off a slack bowstring as he gazed at the naked women approaching him. His arousal was instant. He took in her figure and entrancing golden eyes, not noticing her thinness or panting breath as his groin responded.

Her long white hands took hold of his furs and pulled them apart, revealing his sparsely haired chest. He didn't resist as she pulled at the drawstring holding his trousers and let them fall to the ground. She rubbed herself against his rigid member and pushed him unresisting to the frozen ground, lowering herself onto him.

They began to move, bound by the magic of lust. The pace increased until, with a gasp he erupted inside her. Still they moved as he fought to control her until she thrust her long fingernails into his throat and all movement ceased. She then collapsed on top of him.

Her breathing slowed. She finally lifted her head and looked down at the face, now a gory darkness of fresh rich blood.

She stood, white and tall allowing the liquid to trickle down between her breasts and drip onto the still form beneath her. The form of the Tuplek was already stiffening with the cold.

'My thanks, Sharman,' she said. 'With your blood I will survive. And with your seed my race will survive.'

Her naked form dropped to the ground, swiftly changing back into the silver-coated form of the female Dire wolf.

She loped off into the faint light of the new day.

Where They Fall

The tower of bones fell.

The cloaked woman pushed a long-nailed finger into the scattered pattern.

'Well, what can you see?' growled the broad-shouldered man, bearded face pushed across the table.

'I see,' the finger moved, 'a skull, moss growing through the eye sockets. It… is…'

'What, you old crone?' His spittle flecked the table. 'Tell me!'

She squinted at his head, before reforming the tower. 'Maybe they are mistaken.'

The bones fell.

Night to Remember

It was a crude artist who depicted an ungainly bird, long legs, sharp beak about to engulf a cocky bird at its feet. The orange beak was open like a rabbit snare, too wide for the small prey, yet it appeared to hesitate from such an action. The artist had rendered the large bird in whites and blacks and orange as if he had a surfeit of such colours, yet the little bird was a clump of grey with a single dot of vermillion at its breast; defiance against adversity.

It wasn't a welcoming sign but it was the only colour on the bland building. It was named the Stork and Wren.

Rain hit under my waterproofs, pushing out of a dark sky with a vengeance, changing my thoughts of making the return journey to 'Sommercote' after my adventure into the wilds of Yorkshire. My thoroughbred made my choice for me as I pondered whether to seek shelter in the dilapidated inn sitting at the crossroads of nowhere. The horse moved into the shelter of the attached barn with an alacrity that nearly took my head off on the door beam. He found some loose hay in a dry corner and remained calm as I removed and hung up his saddle. I briefly noted that the barn was empty before I dashed into the storm for the front door of the inn.

I was greeted by the glow of a small lamp and a smouldering fire in the grate of the entrance hall. A selection of sombre portraits welded to the walls disappeared into an unlit upper storey. The desk facing me was bare, a sheet of oak balanced on scuffed wood.

I searched for a bell but a tinkle of laughter from a corridor to my right drew me. A murmur of voices emanated from a lounge near the centre of the building.

The voices stopped as I stood in the doorway, eyes adjusting to the dim light. Dark-coloured wall hangings decorated a large, high-ceiling room, supporting wooden beams barely standing out in the gloom. A range of comfortable furniture occupied most of the space dominated by a vast fire in the process of devouring a substantial log.

The glow flickering off the people seated around the fire revealed them to be well-dressed and in the process of imbibing sparkling wine from long-fluted glasses. A selection of savouries in deep serving dishes sat on several low tables.

I took a deep breath, preparing to announce myself when I was thwarted in this action.

'Welcome,' a melodious voice rose above the crackling of the fire. 'You have arrived at a most opportune time. Won't you join us? Introduce yourself?'

My mouth dropped as I saw the speaker. I don't know whether it was the light, the circumstance or merely kismet but I was stunned. Never had I seen such a desirable woman. Every one of her well-dressed companions disappeared into her shadow, such was her aura of sensuality. Dark ringlets framed an oval face of flawless complexion, full lips above a small chin leading into the elegant white neck set on graceful shoulders.

Those shoulders shook with the tinkling laugh I had heard on first entering the Stork and Wren as she spoke to her companions, a woman and two men.

'Looks like you have another conquest, Amelia,' said the woman.

'Ah, my aching heart,' said the younger man with blonde hair, clasping theatrically at his bosom. 'Does this mean I have to forgo my promised night of pleasure?'

'Jane, Nigel, please don't embarrass the young man.' Amelia swung back and directed her dark eyes to me. 'Don't be upset by my insensitive companions. Come sit with us. Tell me about yourself. I am in need of some amusement. God knows there is little enough to be had here.' She waved a gloved arm around the room indicating the other groups of people now returned to their own business.

I slowly removed my waterproofs while thinking what to say in view of the invitation. There was no choice. The invitation had been made and I was smitten. I could no more walk away than fly.

'Landlord, take our bedraggled visitor's outerwear, then bring another glass,' Amelia said imperiously to a silent man hovering near the door. I hadn't even noticed him as I entered such was my fixation with Amelia, so held out my coat out until I felt it taken.

She patted the spare seat next to her. 'My, you are soaked. Need some warming up, I gather.'

Her smile filled my vision as I sat.

'Now, who are you, my sweet?' She placed a delicate hand on my knee.

Her cold hand competed with the warmth of the fire. A filled glass was placed in my hand and I quickly raised it to my lips.

She leant forward, the action forcing my eyes to her generous cleavage displayed above her green velvet gown.

'Uh, my name is, uh, Clifford.'

'You from around here?' asked Nigel.

I reluctantly turned my head. 'Yes, my father has an estate in the East Farthings, "Summercote". Perhaps you've heard of it?'

'No, can't say that I have. You, John?' he turned to look at the older man who had been quiet during the whole discourse.

'Wouldn't worry her ladyship if we had,' the dark-haired man nodded towards Amelia and my gaze swung back to the exotic creature.

'Her ladyship?' I asked.

Amelia's bosom heaved as she pressed a pastry into my hand. 'Yes, Clifford, I am a Lady. Fortunately ably supported by my dear friends, although widowed these last few months.' Her gaze swung around her companions who seemed to move closer. 'But I am now able to indulge my whims, such as enjoying the delights of the Stork and Wren.'

'Uh,' I took a bite of my pastry.

'Now, Clifford, can you stay for a while? You're not at the beck and call of your father, I trust?'

My chest swelled. 'I have attained my majority,' I blurted. 'I can do what I want.'

'Ah,' she smiled, her arm creeping around my shoulders, a soft breast pressed against my chest. 'These,' she flung a look at her companions, 'would understand if I sought solace with someone other than them? If I could appease my widowhood and the emptiness of my bed for the delights of a young man, they would approve.'

I could feel their gazes but didn't let it influence or tear me away from the delightful creature beside me. 'Yes, Amelia, if I could be of service, I would be willing to remain,' I answered somewhat pompously.

At that moment the fire flickered, the warmth of the log withdrawing, but I didn't take notice such was the

107

power of the woman with me. She whimpered and snuggled into my neck, my hand slipped delightfully down the contours of her back to nestle against a rounded rear. I had no choice when she whispered into my ear to join her upstairs.

She stood.

'Take a glass with you,' she said, ignoring her companions. 'We may need its restorative powers.'

'Yes, Amelia,' I murmured as I rose, no choice but to follow.

We climbed a long flight of steps but I didn't notice, my gaze firmly directed on the movement of Lady Amelia's body.

The tempest howled outside the window of the large bedchamber as Amelia led me to a four-poster and pulled back the coverlet. I needed little encouragement to sit beside her and let her long fingers begin to unfasten my buttons. There was a scent about her, thick and enticing. I drew it in as I watched her dark velvet gown slither to the floor. She lay back and held out her long white arms.

'Clifford, make love to me,' she ordered her dark eyes drawing mine.

My mind withdrew, allowing my body to react to the temptation before me.

And I spent myself in the arms of that most intoxicating woman I'd ever known. All the passion I was capable of and more was drawn from me until I fell into an exhausted slumber.

A cold drop of water splashed on my head, dragging me from my sleep. It was hard to open my eyes such was the depth of my exhaustion. Another drip convinced me to move my head, the effort nearly killing me. The coldness of the sheets around me added to the chill and I groaned awake.

Water dripped through numerous points on the ceiling, illuminated by light creeping through a narrow dirty window. I gasped and stood naked on a wooden floor, seeking the clothes I knew I had worn the night before. I reached down for my trousers and my light-headedness almost caused me to collapse back on the bed. My wooziness and lack of strength as I dressed kept me from wondering where my companion had gone and why the inn was so cold. But when my boots echoed on the wooden floor I thought had been carpeted then my unease became a panic.

I pounded down the stairs and flung open the door to the lounge, half expecting to see the party still going, but all was cold and quiet with a distinct odour of mildew in the air. I noticed my lumped coat against a wall and quickly pulled it on, vaguely recalling that the landlord had taken it from me the previous night.

'Amelia!' I yelled even as I knew my cry would be futile. 'Landlord!' The slight echo of my voice was the only response. I held onto the door my head spinning, a headache burgeoning as I sought to make sense of my predicament. My throat was sore and dry but I knew I would be having no sustenance at this inn. I scratched for a moment at my neck before turning and heading for the front door, hoping there would be a barn, with my horse inside.

His whinny at my entrance was a huge relief. I briefly scanned the empty structure, noting its state of disrepair before saddling and mounting my horse. He needed no encouragement and soon I headed out into a dull grey morning.

My horse's right hoof crunched on some wooden detritus on the muddy road leading past the inn, a splash of colour catching my eye. I reluctantly dismounted to see what it was. After such a momentous night it was a wonder I retained the ability to be curious.

I bent over a plank of wood split for almost its entire length. I turned it over then took a step back in amazement. It was the sign from the Stork and Wren, lying in the mud. The elongated orange beak was broken apart by the split, riven right through the large bird, while the shard containing the grey wren was lodged deep in the head of the stork. I dropped it back into the grey ooze and mounted my patient horse, grateful to leave that place with my sanity intact.

I went back to that dilapidated inn on many occasions but it was always empty; always silent. I scratch at an itch in my neck that still confounds me while I ponder on the mysterious widow who gave me a night I'd never forget.

The Guardian

A scatter of fragrant woodchips dropped over him, settling snowflake-like in his thick greying hair. A strong, sweetish aroma drifted into his wide nostrils. He smiled as he raised a heavily muscled arm.

'Humph!' he grunted. The stone-faced adze bit into the horizontal trunk of red cedar. His smile disappeared into a sea of wrinkles as he concentrated. Again the adze hit the wood, chipping off a calculated amount. And again.

The elder lost himself in the rhythm of his carving as he slowly replicated the shapes so securely fixed in his mind. A lifetime of skill helped bring life to the form. Soon he replaced the adze with the more delicate chisel carrying a sharp shell edge.

A dark, work-hardened arm wiped his sweat-beaded brow, avoiding any distraction that could snuff the crucial life entering the sacred wood. This, he knew, was the time that generations of sharman had foretold. All had to come together.

The curve of the beak was just so--he'd seen it many times. Then the eye, fierce, pitiless and proud; head unbent, feathers alive, almost fluttering in the drift of breeze that pushed the balsamic notes of the cedar through his head; trunk vibrating to the beat of a wooden heart. He caressed the blood-warm, close-knit fibres. The great claws gripped so hard he could feel their points meeting together, driving through the wooden fibres of the shoulders.

The gaping jaws of the huge bear seemed to respond to the agony of that grip. Massively muscled legs

111

supported the bear holding the eagle. Claws on immense paws threatened to attack and yet defend. The shaggy pelt softened to the caress of the craftman's tool.

The day merged into the twilight of the vast forest, the silence only broken by the scrape of the shell edge. The snip of frost cooled him as he worked tirelessly, serving to signal another cycle.

The days grew shorter as the trunk transformed, until he knew that he could give no more. Still one task remained: the placing.

A complex system of ropes inched the uncarved base forward; the deep hole in the thick glacial moraine eagerly received the offering.

A shaft of sun breaking through the scudding wintry clouds struck the imposing figures standing at the head of the valley. Light appeared to reflect from the eagle's eyes atop the snarling of the huge grizzly, lending strength and purpose to the maker's craft.

The carver took no opportunity to admire his work of many months. He turned his back and entered the silent village. His ears were closed to remembered sounds of his people. His eyes saw that nothing was left of his kin's life. His steps took him through the colourless houses that absorbed any light of the dying day and into the thick forest of spruce and cedar as night took its grip. Only the sacred guardian and its memories remained.

As the years attacked, the eagle's eyes softened, feathers grew dull and the bear's jaws lost their ferocious bite. Still it took the invader time to come; to pass the guardian, to get accustomed to the hair prickle on the back of the neck and the uncanny silence of the vast wood.

On occasion one of them would look up at the legacy and wonder about the vanished people.

The beat of life in the sacred totem lived on.

What is Written

The dark plume was ragged as if the individual barbs had been pulled apart and haphazardly re-joined. It was motionless despite the age of the hand holding it. I counted this as an interim blessing since the pen shielded most of his stern countenance from my view.

I'd seen it many times before, from the other side of an ancient desk occupied by a scatter of papers, the Master peering at me from myopic eyes fringed by grey eyebrows that had a mind of their own. The small black eyes focussed across a large nose with a scattering of red veins, ungenerous mouth tight with disapproval.

I wriggled on the uncomfortable wooden stool and watched the pen scratching its laborious way across the detention book. Each scratch of the nib on the page was preceded by a long silence, so I couldn't help following the Master's ideas by ear as he marked down my punishment.

The third year of my internship should have been a year to celebrate, over halfway to becoming a full-fledged wizard with enough learning to run rings around the freshers and impress the girls with my maturity. And at this stage the field was fairly open since the numbers had dwindled due to the strict system that the wizard school had in force.

When you entered the elite school you had to sign away any comebacks that should occur through injury, transmutation or even death. Unfortunately, the very nature of magic and its mastery meant that the risks were high, but the rewards were great. The pinnacle of achievement was to be in the service of the monarch of one of the many kingdoms that existed in our great continent, or be admitted into the White Circle where magic was only limited by the imagination or, the one that tickled my fancy, to be linked to the mind pool of the Dragonkin.

I'm getting ahead of myself. Despite the greatness of my aspirations, my immediate problem was the Master before me. Master Faulsurin was getting past it as far as I was concerned. He'd never made it to one of the three fields that all wizards should aspire to and thus was the head of the school where he could ensure that his frustrations had an outlet, namely on those students who came before him.

'Student… ah Pendle,' the pen slowly made the journey from vertical to horizontal. The Master rested robe-clad elbows on the table surface and clasped two gnarled, liver-spotted hands together on which to rest his weak chin. His eyes gradually passed up my perspiring form before focussing on my face.

'Student Pendle,' he repeated as he slowly shook his head. 'I find you before me again. That makes, uh… five times this year and innumerable times in the preceding two.' He slowly turned the thick pages of the detention book.

'I am told that it is because of your inability to settle in class and a propensity to engage in unauthorised experimentation.' Master Faulsurin sniffed and turned the pages back to the original position. 'I have even had it suggested that you are a mite slow, that it takes some time for instructions to sink in. But I'm of a mind to think otherwise.'

He turned and gazed out of the large casement window looking over the ancient wall surrounding the school. In the distance the blue silhouette of the Spire

Mountains beckoned and I fancied I could see one or two shapes swirling in the updrafts.

'So what to do with you? How to make you fully comprehend the seriousness of your continual transgressions, hmm?' He swung around and looked over my nervous form clad in the sky blue robe of a third year.

His face had a slight glow to it, as if he had some kind thought and not the expression that would lead to the ultimate, a dismissal in disgrace to my humble beginnings where I might rise to the level of assistant pig keeper if I was lucky. For, I believed, to do such would be also to admit failure of their teachings at third year level.

I relaxed, prepared to take detention, extra washing and cleaning perhaps. I even stretched my feet out and touched the legs of that ancient desk.

'Student Pendle,' his old voice became firm, 'I have decided to read you what I have written.'

So, I thought, how else would I know what you wrote?

'Ahem.' He cleared his throat as he looked down. 'Pay close attention even if you think you can't understand, for it is in an unusual script.'

I raised my numb behind off the stool just a little to look across the desk but all I could see were the black meanderings of an old man, not any clearly literate writings.

His voice took on a sing-song quality as he slowly read a series of totally incomprehensible words. I listened closely even as I wondered at old Faulsurin's sanity. I was thinking *if that was the best he could do*, when a sudden thought crossed my mind. *He's doing a spell.*

I tensed and prepared my defences, but too late. The sing-song-ing words were reverberating in my mind, running over themselves like the sustaining pedal in a piano. My body felt strange while my head was echoing in tune until nothing else mattered but the sound.

He stopped reading and I realised it had taken me a while to recover. I was aware of Master Faulsurin observing me with a sad expression on his old face before I felt normal once more.

'What now?' I asked, but was shocked when my words came out in a garbled roar. I tried again with the same result. I stood in panic, but my limbs were stiff and I found it hard to move.

I rubbed at my blue robe which seemed to have become very hard but my hand merely scraped over rough hide, a hand which I was bewildered to see had become scaly with black claws in place of nails.

The Master held up an ornate mirror. The face looking back at me was hideous, scaled and blue with an elongated snout. I choked in horror at what I saw.

'Student Pendle,' he said loudly, 'I suspect you are bright enough to know what you have become?'

My mouth dropped open, revealing white fangs and a long forked tongue. It remained open as he continued.

'I know that you have aspirations to achieve entry to the mind pool of the Dragonkin. Further, that despite your intelligence, you cause considerable disruption within the school and amongst the teaching staff. Punishment, it seems does not deter you. So I have decided to provide a new teaching method that will give you the incentive to learn without the mischief that invariably follows.'

I saw a movement though the window over his shoulder. Two large shapes flying just above the tree tops, coming closer. He glanced in that direction.

'Ah, here come your new teachers,' He reached up and flung open the window.

'But?' I roared.

'Time to go, Student Pendle. You are now a dragon servitor and they are your masters.'

Two large dragons, light blue in appearance, came up to the casement window, the wind from their wings causing the papers to fly from the desk.

'But like this, a parody of a dragon?' My voice grated like two stones rubbing together.

'Of course not, my boy,' he laughed, cheeks turning a bright pink. 'The day that you can read the spell will be the day that you return to normal.'

'But, but how can I? It's in your book, here in the school? And I can't read your scribble.'

'That is your challenge. To learn well enough to understand the draconic runes and to serve well enough to be allowed to return to the school.

'Time to leave,' he said as the back of a large dragon appeared outside the window, 'And remember, all you have to be able to do, Student Pendle, is to read what is written.'

The Master gestured mystically with a nonchalant twist of his hand before turning back to the table and ignoring me as if I'd never existed.

My feet moved without my volition, taking me towards the window and the scaly backs that hovered outside.

I tried to see over his shoulder, to snatch a glimpse of the spell, to memorise the words, to do anything to stop what was happening, but the sight only added to my despair. For as I took that irrevocable step to my new masters, I saw the page was blank.

118

The Price

The iridescent light gave her face a ghostly cast as they crept down the tunnel towards the slumbering beast.

'Quietly, my girl.' His beard tickled her ear. 'Won't do to antagonise it, 'cause there's nowhere to run.'

'You could've gone by yourself to give it the gold,' she hissed, her stomach twisting at the feel of the old man at her back.

'Not possible. The dragon requires something warmer, organic. Something like you.'

'What?' She froze as the dragon caught her in its paralysing stare.

'Well, I don't qualify,' he chuckled as he stepped away. 'I'm not a virgin.'

Sense Less

An explosion hit him, bouncing off in a myriad of directions: inwards, down his gullet; outwards, pouring over lips and chin, rolling and roiling up his nasal passages, assaulting his olfactory cells before spilling from his nostrils.

He was caught unprepared. He should have been ready, expecting it. After all, they were masters of their craft.

His left leg twitched, an uncontrolled reaction which continued as his body coped with the invasion. The masters were testing him, searching the depths of his skill, his control. They would know and be relieved at this show of weakness.

While he concentrated, sorting sensations into levels of activity and effect a subtle mustard shade floated past, briefly obscuring the watching eyes. It came on, pressing across his forehead and linking chain-like around his neck. He exerted control, finding the bonding molecules before dissipating the odour to the corners of the darkened room.

There was no relief. The replacement was a harsher, orange note that prickled on his skin and tried to hold him. It pressed on his chest so hard that his lungs were squashed, causing him to panic and lose control for a moment. But he recovered to fire a burst of his own into the rusty haze, matching molecule for molecule, tying them together. A twist of his mind sent it rocketing back in the direction from which it came.

Another, more insidious opponent, appearing as a red mist emerged from the darkness and moved independently, excitedly towards him. It knew what it wanted. It had an incipient memory of success, rarely needing others' help to achieve the control it desired. Many had succumbed, failing to outlast its presence. Only the occasional master had been able to block it. This candidate was untested.

It attacked, pressing where its fellows had tried. A mesh of fine scarlet lines covered his face, linking cobweb-like to form a second skin. It pulsed its most powerful odour to signal a victory.

But he was different, with qualities the masters had failed to see.

He barely had time to breathe. He could give in, let this malicious force take control, drown him in its unfamiliarity, but he'd confronted too many in the past to allow this one supremacy.

He resisted, pulling power from his mind in massive thrusts that flexed the red web in great heaving surges. With an unheard eruption the covering split into a thousand pieces, flying outwards to momentarily obscure the watchers before dissipating.

He took a great shuddering breath and slumped forward.

The masters watched, waiting silently.

He said nothing, just looked up, smiled and lifted the glass to his lips.

The sommelier bowed from the waist.

Twist

The blade slid between his ribs with a polished ease. Blood quickly stained white robes as the victim staggered and slumped to the dusty road, his cry shrill in the crisp morning air. The guards swung around, hands grasping short swords, feet splayed for action. Their master lay before them, his life spilling into the dirt. They gaped as the assassin saluted them with the bloody knife before vanishing into a slash of light impossibly bright against the blue of the sky.

The Patriarch of Sansuma, Ser Regime Expansea, died in the dust on the walk from the Houses of Learning to his home in the foothills of Sansuma. The killer wasn't found.

'Done?' he asked the form in front of him as the light faded.

'As planned, Magus.' The dark-clothed man lifted the wet knife. 'Would you like to see the blood?'

'Don't get above yourself, Dupis.' The older man glanced at a document on the table in front of him before looking back to the assassin. 'Be available. I may have more use for you shortly. Leave the device with me until then.'

'As you wish, Magus.' Dupis reached over and laid a small silver box on the table. He took a cloth from his pouch, wiped the blade clean and slid it into a leather sheath at his belt. 'I had thought to try the taverns,' he said flippantly.

'Don't test my patience,' growled the Magus as he flipped a dismissive hand. 'Go!'

Dupis bowed and slipped past the solid wooden door.

'The barrier,' muttered the Magus, running an ink-stained finger along the document, 'it will soon be down. Then I'll have complete access to that city and its power. Expansea has been dealt with. The last of the guardians... his daughter, uh…' the finger moved down the document. 'Persea, remains. All I need is her location. Remove her and the city will be under my rule. So, I think her death should be less dramatic… an accident? Yes, better that way.' The Magus's head nodded ponderously.

The hood covered her head, grey and anonymous. The robe was likewise pale and indistinguishable but the hands, slim and fine were not. In the shadows nothing was remarkable until an errant shaft of sunlight struck, turning the knuckle of the third finger on the left hand into a miniature burst of light. A gasp, a quick flap of cloth and the display was lost. But not to the vigilance of the Magus's spies scanning the shadows, seeking a flaw, one mistake, a mistake that could mean a life.

A pair of eyes saw the pale figure change from the slow shamble of an anonymous woman going about her business to the hurried purpose of the exposed. He moved off quickly to send word for the promised reward.

Persea's life hung by a thread. Death stalked the streets and she was the target now her father was gone. She had to protect herself.

Dupis held the small silver box, studying it closely. 'So the Master has another task? A mere woman?' he said, flicking the box with a fingernail, causing a dull thud. 'Little challenge there.'

He slowly opened the box to look into the glow that came from within. *My target has been located.* He

123

thought. *Yes, I will do the deed.* Dupis concentrated. The glow grew and his insubstantial form dissipated to flow through the ether towards his victim.

He viewed the world through a mist, as if a thin veil had been drawn across his eye. Figures tended to meld, their identities hard to discern. That was what saved Persea.

One thrust with my blade my task will be done, he thought as he sought to determine which of the forms in the street ahead was his target. *But this should look like an accident?*

The clopping of a carthorse from behind caught his ear; refuse collectors were a necessary evil even in a prosperous city such as Sansuma. *Fortuitous.* He smiled as he pressed against a pile of rubbish preparing the accident.

A slice into the sensitive loin of the horse caused the beast to rear, catching its master by surprise. It broke into a gallop, dragging the swaying dray behind it. Rubbish scattered as it charged towards the luckless people ahead. They dived towards what little cover there was, those that couldn't get out of the way of the panicked horse were left crushed on the narrow street.

Dupis disregarded the collateral damage as he focused on the grey-cloaked form of his victim lying on the cobbles. His gaze focussed, hand fingering the blade as he made his way towards her to make sure of her death.

Suddenly two city guards came running seeking to give aid. They were between him and her body.

'Blast!' he hissed as he opened his silver box. The flash of bright light was only a momentary distraction in the confusion.

Persea shook her head, feeling for injuries as she slowly rose to her feet. One shoulder was bruised, clipped by the edge of the dray, but otherwise no major hurt. She felt along her body, noticing her ring was glowing, before it faded back to the jewel it was. A splash of red caught her eye. Further on another, leaving a trail of blood past a crumpled figure lying at her feet.

'But for the grace of the gods,' she muttered as she skirted the body and scattered rubbish and followed the receding cries of the refuse collector.

She considered the circumstances of the runaway horse, bleeding, certainly injured. 'No accident.' Then the glow of her ring and a flash of impossibly bright light. 'They are targeting me.' The certainty filled her. 'The Magus!' She slipped through the back roads until she reached her small home, wedged between two larger, white-washed buildings in the artisan quarter. She unlocked the narrow solid-wood door, stepped into the dark corridor and leant against the wall feeling the comfort of its familiarity seep into her bones. 'Yet even here I'm not safe,' she murmered. 'Unless I stop that evil I'm dead. And so is Sansuma.'

Here the ring showed its nature. A wall, unprepossessing, became a gap, a passage into a secret void the Expanseas had guarded for generations. Persea, the last of the guardians slipped into the space and stood absorbing the pulse of the city, feeling its healing power while her mind pondered the threat against her.

The ancient magic that had guarded Sansuma for eons always attracted power seekers, those envious of the riches they thought it would bring. As the guardians, her family had always thwarted such attempts. Yet now things were critical. A more powerful man had arisen in the west, stopping at nothing to achieve his desires. And Persea knew she was the only impediment in his way.

She strengthened the wards, hoping they'd be enough to stop the ingress of the assassin using the Magus's revolutionary translocation device. 'Where had he found such a device to operate over distance?' she murmured. 'How can I stop him getting to me?' She spared little thought for the death of her father. He had taught her well. Sansuma's protection was all-important, personal considerations mattered little under such overwhelming responsibility.

She walked to a stone projecting from the floor, insignificant by itself but the focus of power protecting the city. A loss of this power would break the city open, leave it an empty shell. Regime Expansea had known of this man; thought him just another minor despot in the west and paid him little heed. To his cost.

Her mind fought with the situation, understanding her fate if she failed to find a solution. The flash, an after image of a shadowy figure and the panicked horse were clues she could not ignore.

Persea pressed the ring onto the stone. Initial resistance then the crystals melted into the surface, releasing a succession of circles graduating from pinks to pale blues that filled the room. Their spacing tightened until they reached her, focusing on her heart. She squinted, seeking another narrowing, another focus, but there was only one; her father's was gone.

Persea concentrated, reaching through the circles drawing in the power, feeling the city, seeking the disturbance caused by the assassin and his master. The break in the force showed what she suspected: the Magus sitting like a spider in his eyrie far to the west. Yet the links were there. 'Oh why did you not look, father? Why?'

Her eyes narrowed; she could follow a line, a link to his man, a link to this new device. 'Maybe there's a chance,' she said.

'Failed!' The Magus's eyebrows rose into his receding hairline.

'No,' Dupis said forcefully. 'If you'd allowed me to follow my plan I would not have failed. Accidents are just that, accidents. A knife is a permanent solution.'

'Bah! You could talk your way out of anything.' The Master lifted the silver box. 'This device was developed at great expense and uses much power with each operation. Do you even care? Each translocation failure costs!' His long spidery fingers caressed the metal. 'One more chance, Dupis. She is in her rooms, her 'hidden' chamber, unsuspecting, unprotected.' He held out the box. 'Do the deed. Bring me her heart.'

Dupis took the box, giving a slight bow. 'Your wish is my command, oh Magus.'

'Go!'

The circles of light corruscated, colours flickering through pink to blue. 'Ah, he comes.' Persea's eyes tightened as the circles narrowed, hand with the crystal ring gripping the stone column.

A slash of impossibly bright light preceded a shadowy figure. A knife lunged towards her breast.

'No!' Persea's hand slapped the stone.

The circles filling the room snapped together, slicing through the band of light. The look on the assassin's face was one of shock. His dagger clanged as his body slumped to the floor, his life force disappearing.

Persea increased the ambient light with simple gesture before stepping forward towards the remains of the assassin. A glint of silver caught her eyes.

She picked up the silver object and the blood covered dagger before retreating to the stone column even as she opened the box. 'Time is of the essence, dear Magus.' A light grew, impossibly bright. Persea stepped through.

'Back so soon, Dupis. And my trophy?' The Magus's eyes widened as he took in the grey-clad form.

'You?' His fingers flew in a complicated gesture. 'You should be dead!' He half stood from his desk as Persea rushed towards him, dagger outstretched.

Time slowed as the magics warred between the Magus and Persea.

'You can't!' screamed the magician, veins bulging on his temples. 'I will not allow it!'

The circles of light emanating from Persea counteracted the magician's magic. The dagger's point approached his chest.

'No! I will not fail!'

The point pierced the cloth of his shirt. The Magus's eyes bulged as he felt the steel enter his chest and his strength fail.

Persea forced the dagger deep in his chest, gasping as she felt the magician's power fade.'

'And thank you for this gift,' She held out the silver box. 'It really is a most excellent device. Enjoy your time in Hell.'

Persea left the room through a slash of impossibly bright light.

The Phallus of God

Who named the tower the Phallus of God, no-one knew.

Why it was named the Phallus of God was easy to understand.

At the setting of the sun it bloomed, tall and pale. At daylight it disappeared into its lair of dark granitic rock, leaving behind a flat circle of impervious black material with a twice man-height pole, as thick as a thigh in its centre.

Some believed it was the breathing of the planet that caused the movement. The warmth of the earth and its expansion in daylight hid the tower; the coolth of the night contracting, forcing its release from its rock harbour.

Yet there it stood, extended upwards, its sides pale in the light of the moon, intriguing and mysterious. No windows. No doors. No points of egress. Just a flared top surmounted by the pole pointing its way to the heavens.

A town had grown around the mysterious tower and pilgrims flocked to it. Talismans were sold, fertility potions and pottery likenesses. A macabre ritual was played out on occasion, enhancing its notoriety.

It was settled by locals, small mean people, dark of skin yet with a canniness that made many pilgrims keep their hands on their purse. The people had been in the region for generations, calling themselves Phallaceans. The name of their town, Phallacea.

As the economy of the region improved, trade to Phallacea increased. Roads into the town were now metalled with crushed granite; new establishments grew in size and quality. And a religion began. And the Phallaceans prospered.

The wealth of the region attracted envious eyes. Rumours began: the Phallus of God was made of precious metal; it delivered motes of health and long life within its orbit. Space within the township became a premium and so the town became a city. All manner of people were attracted to the gold rush that Phallacea became.

The city Elder was Buccna, a taller Phallacean whose winning smile with white teeth gained much allegiance. A deep purse and many sycophants usually swayed those who wavered in their support.

Priest Narthura, long platted hair outlining a dark face with deeply sunken eyes shadowed Buccna's side, always attentive, always an unnerving presence. His influence on the Elder was uncertain but together they made a formidable team to rule the city. For Phallacea was a religious city where the locals kept a tight hold on the economy through the worship of the Phallus of God. The priestly sect wore dark robes though their leader, Narthura, was said to have a reddish caste to his – *better to hide the blood* it was whispered.

Originally it was a punishment for murderers and thieves, a good way to get rid of the detritus that affected the society. A goat tethered to the pole for a lark, to see if it would survive on the tower during its nightly journey, had vanished when the tower retracted to its lair. An enterprising priest tied a thief to the pole - he was gone the next morning. Thus the practice became commonplace.

Soon it became a celebrated event. Money changed hands. Murderers, thieves, even wanton women were accused with the cry 'Let God judge'. The tower took many to their spiritual reward on its nightly journey.

The few who spoke out about the Elders or the priests that ruled the city were all too often accused with convenient evidence and made to take the one-way journey. Fear ruled and Phallacea, with Buccna's leadership, made sure it stayed that way.

The Elder and the priest shared a long two-story mansion set with clear glass windows that caught the sun and the nightly transition of the tower. A round room surmounting the building became the ritual room. From here priest Narthura would address the crowd when a punishment was to be made. He could sway the crowd with his dark charismatic form and modulated voice, extolling the virtues of the religion and the obvious presence of their God, while denigrating the character of the next sacrifice.

Offerings poured in, trouble was easily vanquished and life was good.

Narthura was relaxing on a soft couch, gently encouraging a young acolyte to be more enthusiastic in her ministrations to his naked form. He was nearing fulfilment when he heard a tap on the door.

Blood suffused his face and he screamed at the intrusion. The tapping stopped.

'Continue,' he gasped, pushing the dark head back onto his lap.

'Ruined,' he muttered as he failed to re-capture his mood. He stood quickly, forcing the woman to stumble to the carpeted floor. 'Get my robe!'

He strode to the basin, quickly washed, then held out his arms while acolyte slipped the robe over him.

131

Narthura arrayed his plaits over the collar and moved to the door. 'This had better be worth the interruption or the tower will have another sacrifice this night.'

A black-clad form lay prostrate outside the door.

Narthura kicked a silk shod foot into its head. 'Well!'

A white face craned up at the priest. 'Uh, there's unrest, your eminence,' he croaked.

'What?'

The figure pushed up to its black clad arms. 'A revolt in the traders' quarter.'

'Traders' quarter?' His mind flicked through the implications as he impatiently gestured for the messenger to rise. 'Who's causing this?' He looked at the man's blank face. 'Never mind.'

Narthura pushed past his underling and hurried along the stone-lined corridor towards the Elder's quarters. He thrust open the door.

Buccna raised his dark face, eyebrows knotted. He sighed and put the scroll on the side table. 'Another urgent matter that couldn't wait for the normal courtesies, Narthura?' He looked pointedly towards the open door.

'Enough of that,' Narthura said, dropping into a soft seat. 'Have you heard of a revolt, an uprising from the traders?'

'An uprising? Do you mean friction with the traders, led by one Hespolder?' He placed his fingers together in a steeple. 'Then, yes, I have.' He clapped his hand together and a small dark girl dressed in a filmy brown shift appeared in a narrow doorway. 'Drink?'

Narthura nodded.

The girl disappeared.

They waited. An angled light entering the windows along the length of the room showed that the day would soon end.

Another sacrifice would be good, thought Narthura. The girl returned with two glasses which she placed on the table. He watched her appreciatively as she hurried off.

He picked up a glass and took a sip of the bitter alcoholic liquid before finding Buccna's eyes appraising him.

'I believe you think you've found a solution to the effect Hespolder appears to be having on this city. It wouldn't be the Phallus of God, by any chance?' A smile creased Buccna's lips, allowing a hint of the white teeth to appear.

'I think it's appropriate to remove such people before they rise to a level that may threaten us.' Narthura looked carefully at the glass, finding interest in a small imperfection. 'A matter of their influence increasing beyond their individuality. Best it be snuffed out before it becomes a revolution.'

He looked over his glass at Buccna.

'I concur,' Buccna said taking a sip of his drink. His eyes strayed to the narrow doorway. 'I believe you can find your own way out?'

Narthura stood and hurried out, focussing on the next stage of his plan.

The crowd roared both its approval and dismay as Trader Hespolder was tied to the pole on the Phallus of God. The sun was sinking in the west and soon the nightly transition of the tower would occur and the fate of the trader who challenged the God-given right of the priests to administer appropriate rule for Phallacea would be decided.

Narthura frowned at the mood of the crowd and its lack of usual fervour before he saw the thick-set trader

133

looking up to where he stood. He smiled down. Another impediment would be removed. So easy, so simple to conjure up evidence to show treachery and unbelief – enough for the perpetrator to be sent to the judgement of God.

The sun set and the tower began its journey. Narthura watched from the ritual room as a stoic Hespolder slowly rose into the night. It was a sight he never tired of, the growth of the tower like an asparagus spear rising from the earth, smooth and inexorable, permanently taking away a piece of human flotsam.

Despite himself, Hespolder was curious rather than scared as he slowly rose with the tower. The satisfied visage of the priest slipped from view until the city lay patchwork-like beneath him. He could see the buildings housing the men and families of the traders a distance away, separate from the areas firmly under the control of the Elder and his ilk. He hoped that his wife and two children would be looked after well enough by the traders' co-operative; after all it was he they had elected as leader to try and break the hold Buccna and Narthura had on Phallacea. As long as the traders stood together they would be alright.

He squared his solid shoulders and briefly tested the ropes holding him to the pole. *The only use of the ropes now is to stop me from falling,* he thought, looking around his small platform, its rim just projecting over the length of the tower. It slowed to a halt. A faint wind ruffled his hair and the light from a waning moon lit his ruddy features.

I wonder when it will happen? He glanced up, following the line of the tower but it was merely dark with a number of stars pale in the moon's light. There

134

were rumours of course: people disintegrated in a blaze of light; God's mouth snatched the sacrifice from the pole; strong winds from the heavens blew the victim away. No-one knew and the perpetrators didn't care.

Hespolder noticed the pole he was secured to growing warmer and vibrating. *Not already?* He closed his eyes, waiting.

Narthura watched through the night, interrupted only by short breaks for food, drink and pleasure. It was near morning and still he wondered about the mechanism that ensured the disposal of people like Trader Hespolder. The precise moment that a living being disappeared, ejaculated to the convenient god, could never be ascertained but a faint flash of light around the middle hour of the night confirmed to him that an unknown power had been operating.

The first light of dawn finally touched the pole of the tower as it retracted, its edge fitting smoothly in its granite lair, the surface clean with no residue. The trader was no longer a problem.

Still a puzzle, thought Narthura, but one we can live with.

He scanned the early morning crowd in the surrounding streets noting some signs of anger and agitation. *Problems that can easily be dealt with*, he thought and went downstairs to his bed.

'It appears that our weeding out of the troublemakers hasn't been effective, Narthura,' said Buccna as they were scanning accounts several weeks later. 'Our tax revenue has fallen, despite a steady increase in people entering the city.'

135

'I'm aware of that,' said Narthura digging his finger under a thick plait. 'There's only so many that can be got rid of by the tower and it takes time to fabricate evidence. They have become more devious in their opposition.' He extracted a small insect and cracked it, aware of his colleague's distaste.

'We have to make it work more effectively. Double the number on the pole. Destroy any sign of revolution.'

'I have thought of that, Buccna, but there's an increasing risk involved. Several patrols have been attacked and even I have had a missile thrown at me.'

'I heard. A cabbage!' he laughed, then his face grew hard. 'Just do it, Narthura, for we both have a lot to lose.'

Attendance at the ritual decreased despite more sacrifices made to God. A curfew became necessary and soon the streets were deserted by nightfall, the only movement being the patrols, with the ominous presence of the tower overshadowing all. The traders had been quiet and the joyless city continued to function.

Narthura pulled at his hair in frustration. It was harder to pin evidence on trouble-makers, indeed it was hard to determine who they were. Worst of all, the populace recognised the farce of the ritual. Their belief in the God was virtually non-existent and revenues were down.

'I've had enough, Buccna!' He strode the carpet in the Elder's room. 'It is I who has to put up with the retaliation of the people but it is we who have to find a solution to their rebellion.'

Buccna's face hardened. He stood and walked to the window. 'Fine, my friend, I can see I'll have to assist more overtly, for the task appears to be beyond you.' He held up his hand to stall Narthura's retort. 'We have to organise a demonstration of God's power, cower them into submission. The mere removal of those dissenters is not enough.'

Narthura paused in his pacing. 'Yes…'

'We have to show our power, our linkage with God or all we have established will be lost.'

'You're mad! We both know that there's no such thing. So how can we possibly show it?'

'Leave it with me. You will know soon enough.'

Narthura left, shaking his head. He truly felt Buccna was losing his mind.

He did more than shake his head when Buccna outlined his plan.

'Never!' he shouted. 'I won't do it!'

'I think it is needed,' the Elder said quietly.

'The answer is obvious then,' retorted Narthura, his face still red.

'Alas, my agility is not what it was and I could not carry it off. You, on the other hand…'

'Why not get one of the others? There's any number who would put their lives at risk at our order.'

'True,' nodded Buccna, 'but think of what it will mean. Do you want one of our underlings to take all the glory? For should it succeed, as I think it must, you will become unique, a man anointed by God. Your position will be unassailable.'

'Bah!' Narthura shook his head. 'There must be another way.'

The Elder slowly shook his head. 'I don't believe so, my friend.'

Narthura dropped to the chair and took a large drink from the cup sitting on the table. After a moment he said to himself. 'Yes, it could work, but only if we pick the right night and have a suitable distraction.'

Buccna smiled.

The crowd built up, standing ten deep in the square. Buccna stood in the ritual room holding everyone's attention. His gestures were theatrical, his words eloquent. Every so often he pointed down to Narthura whose dark form was tied to the pole on top of the Phallus of God. A small body of priests stood in close proximity, while the remainder of the crowd stood well back, kept there by the guards.

'There!' he pointed to the priest. 'There is a man who is willing to risk all to talk to God. And why, why does he do this?'

The crowd stood silent looking between the Elder and the bound form of Narthura.

'No-one will answer?' Buccna glared down. 'He does this for you! He does this to remind you that you are straying from the ways of God. That God is all powerful and you need to return to the fold.'

A murmuring gradually filled the square.

'So he will ascend on the Phallus of God. He will address God. And he will come back from a journey that no-one has ever returned from. And he will be blessed by God.'

The shadows slowly lengthened and the square darkened. The tower began its journey towards the heavens. Narthura's figure stiffened as the tower rose, his face hidden within the hooded cowl of his black robes. The moon edged its way above the city.

The crowd waited until the dark figure finally was obscured by the slight overhang at the top. There was no

138

curfew that night as everyone had been ordered to the square to watch this momentous occasion. Moonlight finally brought light to the scene.

It was important for their plan that everyone was in the square where their view of the top of the tower was obscured. Anyone at the height of the ritual room might have noticed the dark figure of the priest wriggling free from his bindings and his black robe slipping off to reveal a white robe beneath. Narathura fastened ropes to the overhanging rim and gradually slipped over the side to wait, pressed against the tower – the pale sides making him invisible in the light of the moon.

Buccna called to the crowd to give thanks to God just as the priest successfully manoeuvred into position. With their attention on him no-one was aware of what had happened.

The crowd prepared to wait out the night. Buccna settled into a comfortable chair in the ritual room and raised a glass towards his partner perched high on the tower. 'Here's to our success,' he murmured.

The night grew cold. The moon hovered overhead in a cloudless sky. Midnight came and went. A brief flash from the top of the tower caught everyone's attention. A buzz ran through the crowd, expecting the light signalled the end of the powerful priest.

Strange, thought Buccna, *there's no-one on the top, tied to the pole so it shouldn't have lit up?* He stood and moved to the window, trying to catch sight of Narthura.

A scream sounded, loud and long. A figure, white-clad, falling from the tower hit the ground with a thud. People rushed forward.

'The priest. He's dead!'

The guards forced the crowd back as Buccna came hurrying up. He groaned when he saw Narthura's broken body, blood already staining the white robe.

'His robe's turned white!' exclaimed someone. 'God's rejected him!' yelled another. People took up the cry, forcing the Elder to retreat to his mansion. When he appeared at the window a flurry of missiles hit the side of the building. A well-aimed rock shattered the window and he fled into an inside room.

What went wrong? Why did he fall? How can I regain control? Such thoughts filled his mind until the first rays of the sun hit the tower.

The Phallus of God began its descent.

Hespolder blinked, trying to adjust his eyes to the scene below. Recollection nudged his brain, pushing through his memory of the incredible technology he had experienced. The gods had spared him and given him a glimpse of their powers. He witnessed their anger at seeing the distress of their people as the rulers denied them and sought to glorify themselves. He understood where he was, why he had returned. The gods had selected him to right their world. He grasped the transit aerial and held on while the relay tower descended into its housing.

He recognised the bloodied figure lying on the ground, surrounded by priestly guards. He heard the roar of the crowd and noticed the shattered windows of the mansion. He saw the white-faced Buccna trying to defend his position and placate the crowd's fury.

Hespolder smiled and adjusted his golden raiment. He stepped away from the Phallus and raised his arms to the sky, quietening the crowd. The old days of worshipping a false god were over. The new age of enlightenment was about to begin.

141

Treasure

Travel towards the closing day, westward it lies
Only those of intrepid heart can take the trust she hides
Never give the chance to her, take it and then run
For if you tarry, if you fail, you'll never see the sun.

The hand wouldn't open. It was clenched tight, knuckles white.

'Nothing for it. Break 'em!'

The grizzled seaman looked up to his captain, stern features black against the westering sun. 'But Cap'n, she's too pretty t' spoil. Isn't there another way?'

'You questioning me, Silas?'

'But she's a lady, Cap'n. See her dress. Real lace. Even her face's a lady's face. And the crabs ain't even touched her skin.' He licked his lips as his eyes roamed the body lying on the sea-washed cobbles at their feet.

'I can see you'll continue to defy me less I spell it out.' The broad figure leant closer. 'She's the secret; she's the key, the one we've been searching for these long weeks. Now break those fingers, be they a lady's or not. I must see what she's hiding.'

'Aye, Cap'n, aye,' he muttered as he grasped a pale finger and twisted sharply.

'Crack!' the sound echoed as the finger snapped backwards, exposing a portion of the small pale palm.

'Let me see,' growled the captain, pushing the smaller man aside.

The hand lay away from the blue-lace covered side, a tracery of veins clear through the translucent skin. He prodded at the palm, squinting under the remaining clenched fingers.

'Bah! Nothing. Again!'

Silas groaned as he picked up the delicate arm.

'Crack!'

'Nothing. Again!'

'Crack!'

'There! Something's there!' The bigger man wrenched at the hand, causing the body to move in response. He thrust a thick finger into the space under the remaining finger and thumb and levered out a metal object.

'Ah!' The man's face wreathed into a cruel smile as he lifted the small golden key into the wan light of the sinking sun. 'So she had it, hiding it, causing me to chase her all this time. But no matter, with this key I'll unlock the box and be richer than Midas himself.'

'We,' coughed Silas, standing a pace behind the Captain, still crouched at the dead woman's body.

'Uh? Don't get ideas above your station. Now back to the ship. We sail at first light.'

'What about...' Silas pointed at the slender blue clad form. 'We can't leave her here; she's too pretty.'

'You and the crew will have to forget about having her aboard. She's just flotsam, now. The crabs will pick her bones this night. Now move.' He stood and strode off along the cobbled stones to the two-masted pinnace pulled up on shore.

Silas took a lingering look at the woman's body, her long dark hair spread like seaweed from her pale face, one arm outstretched with three broken fingers incongruous on the perfect form, before he hurried after his Captain.

143

The lamp flickered, highlighting the eager faces gathered around the wooden table in the small cabin. The key glittered golden in the light.

'Hey Cap'n, be able to afford more'n this swill when we get to port,' said Silas as he took a swig from his mug.

'Don't get too ahead of yourselves, all of you.' He glared at the five seaman sharing the celebratory rum. 'It's been a long chase and we were lucky her boat foundered when it did or there'd be no key, no treasure.'

'And her holding the key in her pretty little hand just fer us to take,' a beetle-browed man laughed over the rim of his mug.

'Enough, Pisani,' snapped the Captain. 'That woman led us a pretty chase. Now it's up to us to get back and take what we've been after.'

'Don't know the counting house'll see it that way, Cap'n.'

'Whether they do or don't, we have the key, Silas.'

They looked down at the golden object as the bottle was passed around, each thinking about what led them there, to a cobbled beach on a deserted shore and what had led the keeper of the key to run.

'Yer don't think the rumour were true, then?' asked Pisani nervously shuffling his feet.

'Blast yer! Why'd have to bring thet up?' yelped Silas.

'No.' The Captain nodded to the key. 'He's right after all. Just putting out what we're all thinking. And I can't explain it either. No reason for her to run. No reason to make it easy for us, neither.'

'Said she's linked with the devil!'

'Shut up, Silas,' Pisani's eyes rolled whitely as he glanced around the room, the flickering shadows from the lamp seeming life-like.

144

'Get another bottle,' growled the Captain to the squat crewman near the door. 'Be our last drink before we sail on the morning tide. I want you all ready. The sooner we're away from these benighted shores the better.'

The tide turned and the rippling waves began to cover the exposed cobbles, moving up towards the blue-clad form lying arm outflung. Crabs and other carrion eaters moved with it, seeking anything edible yet even these unfussy scavengers moved around the body, not seeking the choice titbits on offer.

The same waves rippled under the hull of the beached ship, giving a prelude to the vessel recommencing its return journey.

The sailors dozed fitfully, befuddled minds uneasy, as the ship trembled with the slap of the waves.

A sound echoed, incongruous on the dim shore, once, twice, three times. The fist uncurled, whole fingers lifted against a dark sky and the form rose. She stood, tall, swivelling towards the black silhouette of the ship.

A delicate foot stretched out, then another, the slight breeze ruffling the lace around her body as she glided towards the vessel with its sleeping cargo; a clattering swarm of ten-legged creatures followed.

No-one saw the golden key re-enter the pale palm. No-one heard the flood of carrion eaters pour over the side of the beached ship as they searched for food.

No-one woke to the new dawn.

Gold is not only in men's hearts, it's also in their eyes
A key to all they want is all that they desire
But when that key is locked secure and forcibly attained

Life is what they hope for and death is all they've gained

The Lure

I'd never have done it but for two reasons.

As an employee of Esk Steam Drilling I put up with the conditions in the compound which covered around ten acres in the centre of over eighteen square miles of verdant rainforest in the disputed region of the African Congo. Esk dutifully kept the region well patrolled and bribed the appropriate officials. The humidity, high security and long hours were only made acceptable by the growing bank account in old England and the promise of a large payout at the end of my stint.

The work for an engineer was predictably mundane unless something broke down, or the fuel was a poor batch. The engines were large but relatively simple with huge boilers, drive shafts, pistons, valves and condensers. They pushed fresh air down the mines and provided motive power for everything from drilling to the lifting mechanisms. All-in-all a routine, easy sort of job.

Then the investors increased security dramatically. When we left the compound after our two-weekly shift we were subject to a body search. Not so bad for a male like me but the few females had it tough. The final indignity due, they said, to increasing thefts of uncuts, was the random body cavity search. My view was irrevocably altered when the large Goth in charge, Herr von Helebore, took delight in searching me.

The other reason, not immediately apparent, was a personal discovery. I had noticed the natives used to burn a particular liquid fuel when worshipping their local deities. Though it was only produced in very small quantities from a local tree it had some singular features:

it burnt slowly, yet had a very hot flame. To a steam engineer it offered an exciting possibility, especially if you were a tinkerer.

Mosquitos whined unceasingly above my head as I worked, their sound broken only by the deep thud of the mine engines and the *ker-chunck* of the guards' steam guns as they fired haphazardly into the verdant forest; whatever animal that deigned to reveal itself was soon full of holes. But my project kept me focussed as the minute engine, no bigger than two joints of my index finger took shape.

I had stripped off my sweat-soaked hard collar that normal propriety demanded and concentrated. My excuse should I be accosted by Herr Commandant--called supervisor for those not in the know--was that a bearing in one of the mine's pistons was overheating and I was working on a solution. The boiler, pipes, cylinder and the minute reciprocating piston were so cleverly constructed I was tempted to boast about my achievements, but I didn't want to attract attention. Indeed simplicity was the key, for it only had to move the wings in an up then down motion for the part-living, part-mechanical insect to fly.

My predilection to catch the giant moths that frequented the jungle meant that I could proceed with my plan without undue interest from my colleagues and those 'gaolers', laughingly called administrators.

'What have you there, Frederick?' asked Gerald, a fellow steam engineer from the same college as I in the old country.

` *Blast!* I thought as I realized he could see the parts of the engine on my work table. Giant Atlas moth wings of the Saturniidae family lay in a heap nearby.

148

'I'm tinkering, as you well know. Dash all else to do when the engines are operating.'

Loud flapping came from a number of large moths with complex antennae which crowded the fine wire sides of a cage nearby. It drew Gerald's attention and he walked over to peer in. 'Never could understand why you're interested in these things. Just another lot of the creatures that make your skin crawl in this stinking jungle.' He shuddered.

'If you don't mind…' I bit my tongue as he wandered back and pushed a finger into the metal pieces I had in front of me.

'That's a boiler, isn't it?' he moved a miniature cylinder. 'How did you make it that small?'

'Rolled plate, extra thin. Tricky, particularly getting the seal right.'

'What about…?'

'Please, Gerald, I'm doing something intricate and it needs my concentration.' I pointed to the wings.

'Oh, really?' he said, 'It's not very appropriate for an engineer. You should be sticking to what you trained for.' With a dismissive flick of his hand, he sauntered off to another part of the workshop.

I briefly thought that he might report me for doing work that didn't seem company related then realized he hated the administrators as much as I did. *If only he had realized what I was really doing.*

I took to taking a live female Atlas moth and several pupae out with me on my rostered time off. At first the guards were suspicious. Herr von Helebore even took delight in squashing one or two specimens and checking their body contents, despite the insects being too light to be containing any contraband. Eventually they seemed to

149

regard it as part of my eccentricity--most of us were a little crazy working in the jungles of Colonial Africa.

I was inside my hut in the sleazy border town just out of Herr's jurisdiction. I had set up a wire-covered box against a window inside my bedroom, leaving a small gap in from the outside. I placed the female inside the box and waited. As night fell the conditions became oppressive with crushing humidity and heat but soon the first of her suitors came calling. Huge male moths, their wide antenna picking up the waft of pheromones from the receptive female, slipped through the narrow gap and into the room. I jumped with delight even as a metal clad security vehicle puffed by on its way to the Esk mines as I realized my scheme had a good chance of working.

For once I couldn't wait to resume my two-week shift. I had left several female pupae in the box, their emergence timed to occur near my return. I even smiled at Herr von Helebore as I passed through the check point, his gimlet eyes, shadowed by the peak of the metal helmet, narrowing at my unexpected levity.

By now I had a number of the miniature engines constructed, each firmly attached to two pairs of collected moth wings. All I now needed was to collect a number of male Atlas moths.

I worked late into the last night of my shift, having again fobbed off the increasingly suspicious Gerald. I carefully removed the head with its large antennae and the sexual organs from each male moth and fastened them to the forefront of the mechanical insects. The contraption, capable of carrying the payload I had fixed behind its miniature boiler, would be guided by the antennae acting like small rudders and driven by the most primitive of needs, sex. I expected the head and boiler would operate long enough to cover the distance to my hut.

150

I lit each flame and waited impatiently for the steam to build. Before long the great wings were beating in time to each movement of the piston. I was then able to carefully release them into the night sky on the appropriate heading. I could hear the small *chug chug* of each engine before they were lost in the cacophony of the creatures of the dark.

My security check as I left next day was thorough. I swear that Herr von Helebore kept his metal gloves on while he explored my nether regions as if he suspected I was up to something. I kept myself under control with the thought that I'd never be coming back if my scheme had worked.

I burst into my hut to find the bedroom full of large male moths clinging to the peeling wallpaper covering the walls or flapping ponderously across the room in search of the elusive scent of the ripe females. I bit down on my elation as I searched through the insects to find the familiar shapes of those I'd constructed. I began to think that I had failed, alarm running through me as I realized the implications of any being found by the authorities. When I rubbed the accumulating sweat from my eyes I fancied I could hear air escaping from a steam engine. I pondered on this since I realised that the miniature boilers would've been exhausted and so silent. I gasped as the *chug chug* grew louder.

The gush of steam exhausting from a large boiler and slamming of iron doors prompted me into frenetic action. I had been betrayed and had mere moments to cover my tracks.

'Herr Frederick,' boomed the Teutonic voice of Herr von Helebore, 'I vould not haff expected this of you. You haff been very naughty, I tink?'

I looked up at the profile of the giant German in his steel spiked hat filling my doorway and attempted to calmly raise an eyebrow. 'What is the meaning of this intrusion into my private life?' I prevaricated. 'Surely your jurisdiction doesn't extend this far.'

'Ah, but it does, Herr Frederick,' replied the compound's commandant with a hollow laugh in his voice, 'especially if it involves theft uf company property.'

'What do you mean?' I replied, stepping back to sit on my bed.

'You haff, I tink been smuggling uncuts from the mine. Usink these repulsive creatures if I am not the mistake to make,' he gestured at the flapping moths all around him.

I naturally protested at my innocence but the smug look on his face made me very concerned for my immediate future.

'Gentlemen!' von Helebore called. He stood to one side as several large Huns pushed into the room and saluted him. He pointed to the flapping moths covering the walls and floor. 'Destroy zem, destroy zem all und bring me vhat you find.' He kept his eye on me as his men knocked the moths down and turned them into pulp with their heavy boots.

Herr von Helebore's satisfied look gradually faded as the men pushed through the remnants of the moths and failed to turn up anything untoward. 'Vell?' he shouted, 'vhat haff you found?' His face turned a choleric red as he pushed his booted feet through the bloody green pulp. 'Nothink? Nothink!'

He thrust a sausage-like finger into my chest, forcing me back a couple of paces. I didn't dare change my expression in response to his frustration, I just waited.

152

'Don't tink you haff got away with anytink!' he spat as he and his men turned to leave the room. 'I'll be vatchink you.'

I waited until I heard the vehicle's engine build up a head of steam and move off. I lit a candle and slipped quietly out into the garden. To my relief, outside the bedroom window I found half a dozen of my mechanical moths where they had fallen unable, due to their inflexible bodies, to enter the narrow gap that the live moths had.

I crouched on my haunches and relieved each contraption of its payload until I had six large uncut diamonds in my hand. I buried all but one of the machines, keeping it as a reminder of my skill and ingenuity in fleecing the large corporation of its valuable uncuts.

I permitted myself a quick smile as I thought of the even larger bonus I would now receive as a result of my skills. A hiss of steam from a company vehicle patrolling the nearby border made me flinch. But as I hurried into the wreckage of my rooms to pack I knew that soon I would be far away leaving von Helebore trying to protect his own body from what the company would force *him* to endure.

The Queen's Prize

'Cudoooshaaaa! Cudoooshaaaa!' Light gleamed on the pistons in the oil-impregnated crud of the pits of the giant hanger. Bulbous eyes amplifying this light watched flat multi-legged creatures scurrying purposefully in the depths. It straddled a pit, waiting, timing each strike in synchronicity with the sound. Nothing noticed the death of each insignificant creature as its blood joined others via the rapacious maw.

After a time gears clicked, cogs whirred and steam hissed; a black-stained shape lifted in the gloom and continued its stilted progress in the dark, the blood of the little creatures barely satisfying its needs. And it needed more.

'You sure you replaced it?' Thick glasses perched on his nose. He delved into the workings of the machine. A large valve and assorted metal pieces lay scattered on the bench.

'Yes, Doc, I did everything required.' The slim figure rubbed a grease-streaked arm across its nose.

'What about the metal? Was it flawed?'

'Checked and no, it wasn't flawed. Did the vanes too, in case you were going to question me about that.'

The bent back tensed and the old scientist twisted his grey-haired head to look at his assistant. 'Don't get snappy, Freddie. We have to be sure it'll work. I have to question.'

'Well, you don't have to go down there, into the slush pits for any lost piece. And I don't fancy going there especially since the accident. Poor Joshua disappeared

154

when he was searching for the General's armature. As if he'd lose such an important piece in the pits!'

'If this doesn't work there'll be no project and we'll be out of the competition; one fewer in the race for the Queen's prize.'

'Still, what's it worth, Doc? My life? Your life? Let the other fools invent it. Let them invent the machine that'll allow the Queen to fly. Me, I'm too young, got too much to do with my life to investigate the pits. Leave the pistons to themselves. They'll keep working as long as there's enough steam.'

'Herr Drockenfeld is why, young Freddie,' the old man twisted back to inspect the workings of the revolutionary steam engine.

'Herr Drockenfeld,' parroted the Doctor's assistant. 'He'll stop at nothing to beat you and win the Queen's favour. You know what happened to the General when his machine showed signs of working too well.'

'The General?' the Doctor's voice was muffled. 'Never proven. Just an unfortunate accident.'

'Blazes, Doc, you know that's not true. How can a body drained of blood be an unfortunate accident? It was too convenient for the German to remove a competitor, despite his alibi. It's a warning for us.

'So we don't go down into the pits, for it's not safe. Joshua did and look what happened to him – never found. Never found. There are other ways of getting information,' Freddie peered into the cylinder over the Doctor's shoulder.

'Spanner.' The Doctor raised a hand, accepting the tool from his assistant.

'Cudooooshaaaa! Cudooooshaaaa!' echoed dully, covering the scratching sound of the dark shape patrolling the depths.

A feminine form emerged from the gush of water vapour pushing into the room. She rubbed a thick towel across her wet blonde hair, fluffing it while looking over the costume spread across the bed.

She nodded at the particularly striking green dress with puffed shoulders. 'Yes,' she murmured, 'the German will like my costume even if it leaves little space for my weapons.' She dragged a bone comb through her hair and then wriggled into her dress, thankful its whalebone-stiffened bodice allowed her to conceal the twin daggers.

A rap on the door made her turn and push her hands down her slim waist, barely hesitating at the concealed slits to the hilts partially covered by edge of the bodice. She eased her feet into ball slippers and headed to the door.

'My,' his gaze, magnified by the glasses, slid up and down her figure.

'Well, Doc?' she replied to his unspoken question. 'We must use everything we can if we're to get to the bottom of this.'

'I've learnt by now not to try and change your mind.' He proffered his jacketed elbow. 'Shall we?'

She took a deep breath, placed her hand on the Doctor's elbow and closed the door behind them.

'Ach, meine schone Madchen.' The tall, uniformed figure clicked his heels and bent low over her hand.

She looked down on the German's head, distaste twisting her full lips as she detected the sheen of pink scalp through the carefully combed strands of hair. Her expression froze to polite disinterest as he rose and peered at her through a single monocle.

'Meine dear Docktor, where haff you bin keeping ziss delight?' The man's gaze crawled down to her cleavage, unaware of her hand sliding towards her dagger's hilt.

'Herr Drockenfeld, Freddie's life is her own. I have not been keeping her anywhere.'

'Ach?' Herr Drockenfeld leant closer, almost dribbling onto her chest.

'Shall we?' She controlled her voice as she pulled the Doctor around the German and headed into the vast reception hall.

'Careful, Freddie, careful!' he whispered. 'We must circulate, see what we can find.'

'Yes,' she answered with a shudder. 'At least I have the Hun's interest.'

Deep in the bowels of the giant hanger a creature moved, slowly, carefully, always in time to the thudding thump of the pistons as it searched for its prey. It paused, lifting its head, peering upwards to the light.

Several circuits, including a respectful nod to the tiny Queen perched on an enormous throne, led them back to where their principle competitor stood with his cronies, heads almost touching. She grew closer and noticed the stiffness in their postures and the brittleness of their features, the vast array of gas lights in the hall highlighting the glitter of their costumes.

'Metal men,' she hissed. 'They're hardly even flesh and blood.'

'Quiet, Freddie,' said her companion, 'whether they're flesh and blood or not they are our major competition and Victoria will have no hesitation in

157

awarding them the contract if they achieve the first sustained flight. We have our work cut out.'

'Ya, meine leibe Doktor,' she parroted, 'we haf. Now let me be about my business. Assuming he has a heart, I am about to attempt to influence it.'

'Oh Freddie, I wish…' The Doctor's hand dropped away as his assistant stepped in Herr Drokenfeld's direction.

'Ach, Frauline Freddie.' The German's eyes sparkled as he saw the young woman's approach. 'Herren, sich verlaufen.' He flicked his hand at his companions.

Freddie moved into the space they vacated. Herr Drokenfeld's gaze flicked to the retreating form of the Doctor before he took hold of her hand and raised it to his thin lips.

'It iss kind uf you to spend time whizz me, schone Frauline.' He kept her hand as his musty odour washed over her.

'Ah, Herr Drokenfeld, I can recognise an accomplished scientist when I see one. Our efforts pale beside what you have achieved.' She kept her face composed as she leaned away from the man.

Herr Drockenfeld lifted his eyes to her face with an effort and gave a tight smile. 'Then we muss giff you a tour, for zhat iss vat you want, ist es nicht?'

'Oh, I'd like that,' Freddie gushed and moved her hand to his proffered arm. She continued chattering as they left the royal gala to enter the nearby hangers.

The thud of the pistons increased away from the party, the gloom intensified by the relative paucity of gaslights. She shivered, feeling vulnerable in her ball gown as they moved through the huge space towards the

158

assemblage of machinery in the German compound. Freddie had always avoided this area with its continual patrol of Teutonic guards, content to keep to the Doctor's allocated workspace. Others had been less circumspect in their search for the holy grail of steam-powered flight and did some snooping of their own, not dissuaded by the show of force in the various competitors' camps. The fact that accidents and mysterious disappearances had frequently occurred made the Doctor and his assistant keep their heads down.

'Ach, I feel sorry for you, Frauline.' Herr Drockenfeld led Freddie through the gates of the German's compound, ignoring the two immobile men on guard.

Freddie raised an eyebrow, too nervous to speak.

'You see,' he lifted the flap of the canvas structure in the centre of their compound, 'we haf so much invested in winning the £100,000, zhat no-one can stand against us. There haf been zhose who haf tried. Well, zhey are no longer a problem. Others?' he smiled.

'Schnapps?' he gestured to a small table which held a clear bottle and glasses.

She nodded weakly.

Freddie scanned the area, her attention immediately drawn to a dark opening in the centre of the space as the German filled two shot glasses.

'Prost!' he clicked his heels and tossed the drink down his throat.

She took a mouthful, feeling the liquid tracing its fiery path down her throat.

'Another?' He lifted the bottle.

She shook her head, almost regretting the action as the effects of the drink flooded her body.

159

He masked a flash of disappointment before turning and replacing the bottle on the table. 'Now,' he gestured towards the opening, 'our access to ze pits. You know ziss?'

'Yes, we have similar, part of the steam power we all use to drive our equipment.'

'Ja, but it hass another purpose. Listen.'

She leaned forward, looking down into the dark, hearing the familiar 'Cudoooshaaaa!' of the pistons. Then she heard it, a smaller echoing beat with crackly undertones. A gleam, there in the darkness made her forget her caution. 'What the…?'

The sudden tightening of the German's hand on her arm made her lean back. 'You haff meddled for ze last time!' he hissed into her ear.

She attempted to pull away but the wooziness she had been feeling became overwhelming and her legs gave way. She felt Herr Drockenfeld's arms around her waist as she blacked out.

'Uh,' she groaned and attempted to rub her face. Her hand wouldn't move, a clinking sound indicating why. She tried to shift her body but she was rigid. She blinked into an impenetrable blackness as she sought to remember. Then the sticky warmth and her nose told her where she was.

The pits, where so much had happened, much unexplained; where deaths had occurred.

Where was Herr Drockenfeld? Why had she let her guard down and taken that drink? Where was the Doc? All these questions were running through her mind as she sought to get free, but the chains around her wrists and ankles stopped her. She was trapped in the pits, alone, her daggers below her bodice giving her a little hope.

160

Freddie swivelled her head towards a leafy crackling pulse breaking through the thud of the pistons. She strained her eyes to a flicker of light. Something was coming. She bit her lip to stop the inadvertent scream as she twisted and strained her body. Then her eyes adjusted and she saw what was moving towards her.

It was tall and spindly, long legs, large head, bulbous eyes and a needle-like proboscis depending from its jaws. Steam wreathed its body as a heartbeat pulse echoed from its large metallic chest cavity.

It hesitated as she craned her neck to keep it in sight, terrified the clink of her metal restraints would draw it to her. The creature took a cautious step in a hiss of steam until it almost hung over her. She saw the proboscis flicking in and out before it tensed above her stomach.

She screamed and pulled herself to one side as far as the chains would allow. The head plunged down between her stomach and arm, banging the platform she was on. Then it retreated several steps, the light in its eyes flicking on and off. Freddie squirmed frantically knowing she had been lucky to avoid the creature's strike.

A snap and twang released an arm, the side where the creature had struck. It hadn't hit her but it had broken a link of the chain restraining her wrist. The creature hissed, moving forwards as she struggled to reach her weapon.

The clang of her dagger hitting the jaws of the creature was music to her ears. It staggered back while she jammed the strong metal blade into the chain on her other wrist, parting the softer metal with little difficulty. She sat up, working at her other restraints while peering into the darkness expecting another attack.

A musty odour came from the dark behind her before she heard Herr Drokenfeld's screech. 'Mein automann!

Vhat haff you done to mein automann, mein creation.'
Strong fingers dug into her shoulder.

'Bastard!' Freddie snapped, thrusting her dagger at
the German. A satisfying impact as the weapon hit flesh
caused the hand to release its grip.

A lantern hit the ground with a crash. The thud of a
body followed. She leant down in the dark, feeling for the
German's body.

'Dead,' she muttered as she touched the dagger hilt
projecting from the body's eye socket. Freddie gulped,
taking time to search the clothing for a tinderbox. She
pulled one from his pocket and ignited the lamp wick. A
glow slowly lit the surroundings, revealing a macabre
scene.

Long coils of metal piping ran past into the darkness
of the underground pits like loose intestines fed steam
into the engines that ran the pistons. A gleam a short way
off revealed a metal creature oozing a dark fluid from its
jaws into the oil-soaked ground, its bulbous eyes dim and
flickering. Freddie prodded at it with her foot before
punching the remaining dagger into the control panel on
its back. A large gush of steam erupted and the lights in
its eyes darkened.

'Herr Drockenfeld,' she hissed and turned to the body
lying next to the platform where she had been bound for
the creature to feed on her blood. 'You were the cause of
the murders. Now you can lie in the filth where you
belong.'

'Freddie. Freddie!'

'Oh,' she looked over to where a ladder led to a
square of light far above. 'Doc, I'm here. I'm coming.'

She pulled her other dagger from the German's eye,
critically examining the point before wiping it on his

162

dress jacket and re-sheathing both knives in their hiding place.

'Freddie, are you all right? We've been searching for you.'

'Yes Doc, I am,' she answered as she reached the ladder, 'and I suspect we won't be having any more trouble down in the pits.'

Darkness refilled the pits, the smell of death and fresh blood pervading the space below the ladder. The motionless creature suddenly pulsed with a light thudding of pistons, bulbous eyes brightening through a drift of steam. It lifted its head to sample the air.

After a momentary hesitation it rose on its spindly legs and moved forward to feed.

163

Ink of Life

'There!' she stabbed a long finger at a prominent vein in his right arm. 'Use that.'

The man looked at the pretty woman in front of him, bright eyes animated in her pale face, scared at the evil her looks concealed. A red tongue flickering across small white teeth revealed her intensity.

A lean brown hand pushed down hard, immobilising his arm. He stiffened as the glint of the blade caught his eye.

'It begins, my Queen,' said the magister, his wizened face close to the man's arm.

'Ah,' Zynera breathed, her face lit. 'It will record his hidden knowledge? On the parchment as you said?'

'So I believe.' He moved the ancient pen's nib to the blank surface.

'You believe? You said his life's blood will reveal the secret. Are you retracting your word, Pencnem?' Her face hardened.

'No, my queen. No,' he straightened, holding up his hand. 'I am but concerned about the consequences of what we have done.'

'Now! When we are so close!' She pushed her face into his. 'We go ahead. Not you or those simpering fools who advise me will stop this.' She stepped back. 'Proceed!'

Pencnem pressed the sharpened top of the pen into the vein. Almost immediately the instrument began to move. Blood appeared from the nib and the scratch of the pen broke across the harsh breathing of the victim.

The man strained against the ropes that held him to the chair, heaving his body away from his immobile traitorous arm. His eyes bulged as the pen moved. He screamed through his gag when words, in blood, revealed secrets he'd never articulated.

He was the head of his household, yet unable to refuse the Queen's call to attend the council. His holdings, to the distant west of the Kingdom, were far enough to be away from the influence of the avaricious witch and her designs. His word and that of his ancestors were immutable, never to be broken. Yet somehow Zynera had known, had determined that a secret was kept, and found a way for it to be revealed.

Red words flowed. The parchment's long length was partially filled with crusted script. He fell unconscious, his white form slumping against his bindings.

The Queen read while the pen continued its eerie scratching. Her eyes narrowed at her companion. 'We'll soon have enough detail. As long as his words keep coming.'

'I think,' said Pencnem, averting his face from the wasted man, 'that his life will soon run out. If that happens I'm uncertain the spell can be sustained without fresh blood.''

'What!' her voice rang out. 'Don't even contemplate it. Use your blood.'

'But I'm old. I mightn't survive.' His voice wavered.

She smiled bleakly. 'You mightn't survive if you don't.'

Pencnem's face froze. He bowed, slit a main vein in his forearm and held it against the pen. The instrument eagerly accepted his blood as it joined the faltering flow from the man.

The Queen read the words, only partially noticing her wizard's form slumping against the victim. 'Close. So close.'

The pen's nib suddenly scratched dry.

'What's happening? Why won't it write?' She rounded on Pencnem in her fury.

'My Queen,' his voice rattled. 'I am old. My blood gives out. I cannot continue.'

'You must.' Her voice shrilled. 'I must know. What should I do?'

'It needs blood,' he whispered. 'Your blood.'

'Mine? Why not a guard?'

'The spell only for… us… No others'

'Fine!' Zynera bared an arm and took up the blade, hesitating while choosing a dark vein. 'I'm willing to spare a portion of my royal blood, even if others are not. The reward will be worth it.' She sliced into her pale skin and her rich red blood soon filled the quill.

The pen continued writing.

'I can see it,' said Zynera weakly. 'The final detail I'll need. Can't it write faster?'

She leaned against the bodies of her companions, fixated only on the words that flowed redly onto the parchment. Finally her head slumped, her eyes closing.

Soon the only sound in the room was the scratch of the pen. It ceased when its ink ran out.

Love of Music

Fingers, thickened and calloused, caressed the strings eliciting a strident yet melodic sound to echo through the stadium in a primeval pulse. The beat added to the feel of the air, throbbing and pulsating along with 3,000 hearts.

He was lost in his world, following every hit on the strings, adding to the rhythm, allowing the audience to forget and live for the music. He didn't think of himself, his mistakes and his regrets, he just lived for the music.

The sound took him away from his pain. Each hit of the hand, each slice of skin off fingers was forgotten, peeling off pieces of himself to float away like dust in the air. He just lived for the music.

Sweat dripped, soaking his t-shirt, puddling around his belt, pulling life from his body. But he didn't care, couldn't care, the music let him forget. And he had to forget.

The cut of the amps, the fading of the lights, bowing to an amorphous audience brought his mind, his being to the present. The music had stopped him from remembering, but only briefly. He couldn't escape. He wasn't ready to take the ultimate step. He had to face his demons head on. Or so he told himself as he packed up his guitar and stumbled out into the early dawn, his feet following a remembered path.

He shoved the cardboard door and fell across the threshold. Maybe this day he wouldn't remember. He spilt a line of white powder across his kitchen bench and inhaled it through a rolled note. Maybe he wouldn't remember, ever.

A pale oval face, eyes squinting at him hiding in the doorway, ready to put a foot into the river of people flowing past made him want to stay, be content in his refuge but hunger was driving him out.

'Soon, Carly,' he whispered into the shadows. 'Be patient.'

He plunged into that river, ducking between legs, coat flapping, looking ahead. An occasional curse followed him as he bumped and weaved his way to the back of the Maccas. It was important to get there early, be the first to the bins. The best spills had no time to spoil in the sun, no time to be grabbed by other scavengers.

He snatched at a spoiled meat patty with gusto. Meat, real meat not soggy spoiled buns. They wouldn't go hungry tonight. He filled his plastic bag with a range of food, not worried he couldn't identify most of it. He wasn't particular; he had responsibilities.

He took his time going back, away from the traffic, targeting the eddies in the movement of the people where things slowed down, where time made space for his kind.

'Yer got sumfing, Joel?' Her voice was soft and filled him with a warm feeling, making everything he'd gone through worthwhile.

'Yeah. And,' he said to the pale face peeking through the broken slat under the decaying apartment block, 'got some meat too, hardly touched.' He edged down and through the gap until he felt the push of a small hand. He released the bag and watched in the dim light as the waif pulled at the contents. *Like Christmas*. The thought came unbidden. *A time of joy, of fun.* Joel squashed it under the cement of time and pulled his threadbare coat tighter around his thin shoulders.

The months passed, food always a priority, second to shelter. Only Carly's needs kept him going, kept him from finishing his run on the treadmill of life. Then a chance find changed everything.

A broken stave of wood jutted from a torn garbage bag spilling from a dumpster. *No food*, he observed and almost passed it by. A curl of wire caught the fickle light and he stopped, climbed up and pulled the shattered guitar into his arms. *Good*, he thought, *something to keep our minds off our bellies* and put it into his sack.

It became a drug, an addiction in his life. The music soothed him, took his mind away from their hunger, gave him another purpose. He didn't notice their plight if he played. Didn't care what Carly brought to their home under the broken-down apartment block, he just drew on the music.

He found a small corner to one side of the markets and began to play. Carly put down a hat and looked at the passers-by with her big eyes. Their life started to change, better food, drier and less draughty digs.

Joel began to live for the music and nothing else mattered.

The big break came. An offer to join a band, to play his music. Just him. No room for Carly. He had to make a decision. The music won.

They began to drift apart until one day she wasn't there when he came back from a gig. A scratched note said she'd left to follow her path, not his. He let it go. He didn't need her, didn't need anyone, he just wanted to play.

They were performing to bigger audiences now, people wanting them and wanting him, his music.

A harsh face pushed across his vision just before they were due to play. He was picking out a new tune, a trickle of notes like a small stream bubbling over rocks. Strangely it reminded him of Carly; their companionship, her uncomplaining nature and faithfulness. But the manager's gruff voice broke through and dashed the magic.

'Didn't yer know that girl?' a sour breath pushed into his space.

'Huh?' he tried to focus. 'What?'

'That girl. Usta hang around with you a while back.'

'Carly?' he asked thinking it was the first time her name had crossed his lips in ages.

'That's her.'

'What of it?' His heart began to pound.

'She's dead. Dragged her outta the river. No-one knows what happened.' The manager's small eyes seemed to glow with satisfaction. 'Still, shouldn't mean much to yer. It were a long time ago, before yer were famous, weren't it?

'Hey, yer don't look too good. Shouldn't have told yer, especially before yer go on.   Don't let yer punters down, hey.' He patted his bowed shoulder and left the room.

Joel's hands gravitated to the strings and the new tune slowly lifted into the air, louder and louder. The stream trickled as it ran, growing, building into a river, a torrent. But no matter how hard he tried the rush of the music couldn't capture the essence of her soul. She had truly gone and he had let her go.

The thing that mattered most to him had drifted away without him noticing.

170

His bloody fingers caressed the strings pushing the strident melodic sound to over 3,000 hearts, 3000 souls. He tried to lose himself with every hit on the strings, every pulse of the music. But he couldn't shut off her trusting face and Carly's unconditional love; he couldn't close himself off with the music.

The hit of the white powder only intensified his longing, made his fingers slip away as he grabbed at the slim pale hand. He could see her eyes, dark and huge looking back as her form faded from his mind, the blackness growing and driving his craving. Joel jerked out another line of powder for the final hit.

He fumbled rolling the dirty note so dropped his head to the stained vinyl surface and tried to inhale.

A stray gust of wind puffed over the drug, taking it from his reach. He stared at the blank bench top without comprehension until a sound filtered into his brain. Music, familiar and light pushed into his mind until he forgot his need.

He looked up and saw a frail figure outlined in the doorway, holding a guitar.

The instrument was in his hands, calloused fingers strumming the strings, her presence comfortable at his shoulder. He had found what mattered.

Soulsearcher

We were like shop dummies, back-lit eyes, windows to the soul. But it didn't work. We hadn't souls and my hopes of one were zero.

We were triplets and we all looked the same: Asiatic appearance, black fringed hair, cute face, fixed smile trying to win your heart, like a doll in the window who wants you to take it home, live with you, become a fixture, until your fancy changes and you move onto more important things.

I felt I must have been the one in the middle. I would never have been Suze, the girl on the left--too exposed, too open. The right-hand one, Yeo? No. Too needy, wanting to be part of the others. Had to be Kim, the one in the middle.

So I wanted to be different. I needed a soul, that little thing that warms your heart, gives you reason. Stops you being afraid, being alone.

My head was fixed to a stiff, unyielding body. My vision always took in the same faces, the same bodies in triplicate, repeated again and again, all named Suze, Kim and Yeo. The detail varied depending on the brightness--opaque windows high in the roof caused fluctuations in light as the day progressed.

Dust thickened over time but our black hair and 'cute' faces repelled it; something in our manufacture I guess. But time does have its way and my awareness was aroused when a Suze, the name written on her left breast pocket, lost her dress. It just broke apart and fell, adding to the dust.

The only visitors were infrequent, the four legged kind–rats. They usually left us alone as plastics weren't to their tastes, but then a large one, all bone and sinew, began to nestle between my black synthetic shoes. I took some interest, once I noticed the warmth it generated. I found I was able to draw on that warmth, pull it into my body and warm my heart. I kept pulling, pulling until the creature added to the dust at my feet.

I had absorbed its soul.

The rat hadn't given me enough, so I searched for more. Its kind were there in the warehouse, but never still, never coming to where one of their own had perished. There had to be another way. My companions, in their triplicate thousands, gave no help--inanimate plastic, stored and forgotten when the trend for 'cute' companions faded.

I was different. I was growing a soul.

Another warmth revealed itself, but fixed, unmoving. My feet moved with effort, pushing through the dust, manoeuvring myself around many sisters, Suze, Kim and Yeo, stretching in rows across the warehouse floor. I reached a column soaring to the vast ceiling–its base was my target.

I pressed against it, feeling it through my now pliable skin. Its warmth rose into my body, adding to my soul's awareness. I stood there in the dark and dust amongst thousands of my sisters and luxuriated in the feel.

'It's here, the power leak. Somewhere near the back.' The voice echoed through the vast space.

'There should be nothing. It was decommissioned decades ago,' the second voice answered.

'Have to find it. Close it down. Can't waste power. More than our lives are worth.'

'Okay. Okay. That's the directive. Can't let any leaks happen.'

The voices came closer. I withdrew into myself, growing a skin around that beautiful soul. To keep it, protect it.

They passed through the rows of figures with detectors out, two shapes in anonymous uniforms.

I tested my limbs, flexing strong fingers, turning my head, watching them approach. My soul trembled, a delightful feeling. Air squeaked from my throat.

'What's that?' A man's voice rose.

'I can't hear anything,' his companion said quickly. 'Let's find the leak and get out of here. This lot's due for recycling soon, anyway.'

'There's s… something wrong.'

I froze as I saw him pull at his companion's sleeve.

'Where?'

The voice was close.

'There. There's four of them. Not three.'

'So?'

'There's always three. Always been three. See?'

I froze as the light ran across my face and those of my sisters.

'Have a look.'

The light moved closer. I could feel their warmth.

'See the names. Suze, Yeo and Kim. See!' his voice increased in pitch. 'There's another Kim. Shouldn't be here.'

'You're right. Hey, look at the detector. A power surge.'

Their heads bent over the illuminated panel of their instrument.

174

I knew nothing about power surges or recycling, I only knew of the opportunity as I quietly reached out with clawed fingers.

There were souls ripe for the taking.

I wouldn't be alone, anymore.

It Is As It Should Be

A long trill, ending in a high sharp note, was echoed by other song birds throughout the valley. Silence abruptly descended, leaving a background of breeze-rattling leaves destined to fall from the swath of tall birches blanketing the slopes. The faintest of hum from insects competed with the gurgle and splash of a stream feeding its effort to a later rush of waters in the distance. A large black raven flapped its laborious way through the thin air, each beat a thud. It cast a cautious eye on the thin figure standing against a stone wall before uttering a harsh echoing croak.

The figure nodded. 'It is as it should be,' he whispered as if avoiding adding his voice to the symphony of sound.

Brother Meeke rubbed his bald head and turned to climb the rough stone steps to his cottage perched above. As he climbed he ran a hand through the dried marigolds lining the path, rattling the heads. He kept climbing, listening to the slap of his leather sandals on the rock as he passed under the wires of the clothesline and finally entered the weathered wooden door.

He closed the door, the click of the latch sounding loud and looked at the stairs leading to the classroom. 'More steps and another term.' His face hardened.

'The Blessings of Sound to you, my students,' he growled at the teenagers sitting in the rows of wooden desks.

'The Blessing of Sound to you, my teacher,' intoned the students in a ragged resonance.

He slowly sat in his chair at the head of the room and scanned the faces: some bright, some dull; some interested, some not; all youthful. All were dressed in the uniform of military students, grey trousers, dark blue tops with a flap collar.

More potential fodder for the war machine, he thought, his mind closing off from the valley he'd left.

He reached out to a brass bell on the desk in front of him and flicked it with a long gnarled nail. Immediately a mellow tone rang out until the dust motes hovering in the air moved in unison, the very action making them obvious.

The students' reactions varied: several jaws dropped and some smiled except for the three sitting in the back row with their heads together. Brother Meeke frowned and extended his exceptional hearing to eavesdrop.

'Told you,' whispered one, tall and skinny with a prominent Adam's apple.

'Meeke's going over the same old stuff,' said the middle boy, eyebrow lifted in a fat face.

'Think he'd learn more after last term,' chortled the third, grinning through prominent teeth. 'He's getting senile.'

Enough, he thought, I'll tend to them later.

'Your attention!' He said this in a whisper, but the sound grew louder, echoing around the room, building in volume until the words crashed painfully into ears. All students clapped hands over their ears.

Brother Meeke waved a hand and the whisper stopped, leaving a dull silence. 'Now I have your attention!

'You are here for one reason only.' The student dropped their hands and all eyes were on him. 'The Emperor has decreed that all of talent should aid in the

177

war effort. You have shown the rare ability to use and manipulate sound, as I have just demonstrated. If you apply yourself to your studies you will be able to assist our efforts to repel the enemy, for times are dire and we are under constant attack. Our forces are failing and ...'

'I've tried,' he said softly as he paced in front of the three students standing in front of him. 'I've been given an onerous responsibility by the Emperor in time of great need. You, like the rest of the class, have had a unique opportunity to develop a rare and precious talent, one that our community depends on, yet you three squander that chance, consistently.'

A light breeze from the window brushed his face, causing him to hesitate in his pacing, then a whisper of talk caught his ears. *Will they never learn? Too late for that.* He swung around. The students straightened, guilty expressions on their faces.

'No, it appears that you won't take the chance offered you. And unfortunately I can't allow what knowledge you've gained to potentially fall to the enemy. It cannot leave this room.'

'A rare example of sound modulation that you will never be able to repeat.' A vein in his temple wriggled like a live worm as his mouth opened and a deep moan began from the depths of his lungs.

All noise left their bodies in a moment: the beat of a heart; the gurgle of the gut, the rush of blood in veins; the heave of breath; even the sibilant hiss of defoliating skin.

All structures broke down leaving the latticework of their bodies pale and deformed, no longer recognisable as human.

178

Brother Meeke staggered back against the wall, his face a mixture of pain and pity. 'I hope I never have to do that again,' he gasped. 'If it wasn't for the needs of war, I wouldn't.'

He bent over and, with an effort, picked up the three light flaccid bodies, heaved them over his shoulder and slowly descended the stairs. He opened the weathered wooden door, stepped outside and stopped under the wires of the clothesline.

The tumbling thud of the bodies to the stone steps was curious in the silence filling the valley. The friar shook his head and took two pegs from a basket. He lifted one of the bodies and pegged it by its collar flap to the wire before repeating the exercise until three shapes hung in the silence.

He took a step back, pulling his gaze away to drink in the sight of his valley. After a time he heard bird song - a long trill echoing in a sharp note, a breeze rattled the leaves, while insect hum competed with the gurgle of water. A harsh caw of a raven broke through the sounds as its wings thudded through the sky.

Brother Meeke nodded and said grimly, 'It is as it should be.'

Horsenail

The first thing I saw at the bar of the Horsenail Inn was a large, rusted nail lying on the weathered wooden surface. I was touching it with my finger when I felt a presence, a figure, standing in the comparative gloom. I looked up the man's huge frame to the beefy square face topped by a sprinkling of grey hair. He squinted at me through eyes buried in rolls of fat before slamming down a large tankard. A slop of froth spilling onto the drink-stained bar caused me to step back.

'Is that what ya want, pleb?' the barman rumbled, 'or are ya gonna keep staring?'

'I, err,' I mumbled gazing around the empty room with its sagging wooden walls, patches of failed plaster and aging chairs. Even the webs festooning the corners of the ceiling seemed to have been spun by lazy spiders. I fastened on the only bright spot, a well-drawn picture of five intrepid-looking figures on the wall behind him. 'I...was wondering about that picture,' I pointed. 'It looks... out of place, somehow.'

He leant forward, face hard, belly pushing against the bar. 'What?'

I stepped back to avoid spittle hitting my face.

Then his shoulders slumped. 'Ah,' his face softened and he pushed a spade-like hand across his scalp. He took a tankard and filled it from the keg on the shelf behind him then took a large swig.

I tentatively took a sip of mine, trying to find a recognisable taste. The barman sat on a stool behind the bar.

'If ya've got time, pleb, I'll tell ya a story 'bout it,' he jerked a thumb over his shoulder at the picture.

I took no offence at his use of the vulgar term 'pleb', just I settled on my stool. 'Go on,'

He leant forward, resting scarred elbows on the bar and peered into his beer. 'They're all dead,' he said quietly. 'All gone. The picture's all that's left.'

I stared at the picture with renewed interest, seeing the voluptuous barmaid, the lute player and the three warriors or adventurers – a woman and two men. They looked to be having fun in a better kept inn than the one I was in.

'Yeah, they look like they're having a good time, don't they?' the barman said, echoing my thoughts. 'Well, they were then.

'Adventurers all they was, even Besseme, the one with the big tits. She used ta like show 'erself off she did, but underneath she were as hard as nails.'

I studied the picture.

'Yeah,' he said, 'ya wouldn't recognise the place as this here dump, would'ya? 'Course it wasn't called *Horsenail* then. Changed the name when I got back, before things went further downhill. Needed t' do it before the memory faded.'

'Memory?'

'Yeah, and all for the want of a horsenail.' His voice tailed off. I took another sip of the flat, tasteless beer and waited.

He raised his eyes and jumped as if seeing me for the first time. 'Ah, pleb. Ya wants the story, eh?' He took another swig and began.

'It were the King's quest, it were. Gold promised to them who brought back an egg. Thet lot in the picture were me and me friends.

181

'We was down on our luck at thet time but reckoned we knew where an egg should be, where it were hidden. And the gold were too much to refuse.

'We was up early the next day, shutting the inn and leading a supply-laden donkey into the mountains. My head weren't too good from our last night of celebration but the others were in high spirits. Remember telling Besseme to shut it. Got a kick fer me trouble too.'

So the story began and whether it was the beer or the quality of the story telling I soon felt like I was in the actual adventure.

I was leading the donkey, felt the tug-tug of the tether in my broad hand as I negotiated a rough track. Ahead I could see the slim shoulders of the true warrior amongst us, Garoth. Leading him was the whippet-like form of Serah, as quick with words as with her long knife, while just in front of me was Besseme. I followed the sway of her hips with a familiarity I had no recollection of experiencing. And I could hear Lightar playing that damned lute of his without a care in the world.

'Humph,' I grumbled and gave a sharp tug on the beast's tether.

The air was crisp and clean that night like I'd never felt it before. It blew from the mountains, carrying undefinable scents with memories of snow and rain-washed stone. I let it flow over me as I sat by the glowing fire, flickers of light reflecting off the features of my comrades. Lightar played as usual but the notes, for once, seemed to suit the mood. Besseme and Serah were finishing off a fulsome stew as it hung from a tripod over the coals.

I felt truly content.

I woke to the braying of the donkey. The sun's first rays were turning the dark sky to pale blue with streaks of pink and mauve lighting the thin wispy clouds. Garoth was kicking the fire into life and then Besseme banged a frying pan onto the coals. I stood up and wandered a distance away to take a leak. As I stood there I heard the scream of an eagle. I could see it, high and black in the sky. How large it was I couldn't tell but it caused a shiver to run down my spine.

I wandered back to check the donkey, wondering what had caused it to bray. Its body seemed fine, no inflammation or sore spots although it seemed skittish. I heard a clank of the pan moments before the smell of frying ham drifted across my nose. My stomach rumbled in response so I forgot the animal and headed for the camp.

We wandered further into the mountains for several more days, getting to places rarely if ever travelled. The mountains were higher, casting deeper shadows. The sun seemed to be troubled, unable to cast much heat and light. There was no sign of life aside from the occasional scream of an eagle.

I knew we were getting close to our goal.

That night we had a cold camp, rugged up as much as we could. Garoth allowed no fire and none of us argued for it. We knew we were near, near where the egg was supposed to be. Near where no-one had ever ventured.

I woke up feeling like each rock under my blanket had pushed its way through my skin. It took a few stretches to get going. I checked the donkey but all it did was shiver, ripples running in waves along its skin. We headed off, me as usual at the rear leading the beast. No talking and no strumming of the lute. We were all serious that day.

We took a rough path, more scree than trail, which led through a narrow defile in between angled columns of granite. It was shadowed for a long time until we took a turning into a clearing where, strangely, a shaft of light from the noonday sun lit the water-ground stones. A small chuckling stream ran through and disappeared into a dark cavern on the far side.

'That's it,' growled Garoth. 'That's where it'll be.'

They rushed forward.

Then the donkey dropped to the ground, pulling me back.

'Shit!' I exclaimed and went to check what was wrong. I badly wanted to go with my comrades but we needed the animal.

I knelt beside it in the shadows of the walls of granite and felt carefully along each leg. Then I noticed the hoof with a loose shoe. Somehow the horsenail had worked loose and caused the shoe to pivot and lame the donkey. I gritted my teeth to stop swearing.

A sudden screech of the eagle, loud and near caused me to jump as I pulled out the loose nail.

A short while later a distant sound above the noise of the stream drew my attention. I heard the unmistakable clash of steel and knew I was needed. I left the donkey and, pulling my hand axe loose, ran towards the noise.

The sounds muted but clear led into the cavern. I briefly noticed that the tracks of my friends were obscured here and there by other, larger marks as I ran into the dark. I was blinking to try and get accustomed to the dimness when I stumbled over something that gave as I hit it. I felt around and touched the object. It was warm and wet with the smell of blood. My fingers recognised the soft contours of a familiar torso. I sat back on my haunches and took a long shuddering breath.

An ear piercing screech snapped me into awareness and I staggered to my feet to run deeper into the cave.

The glow was bright after the dark coming from an iridescent egg-like object. Then I saw Garoth, our leader, fighting a huge, feathered beast with long neck and cruel beak. As he sliced at its head with his sword a clawed foot ripped into his side, causing him to stagger back.

I yelled, raised my axe and ran at the monster, seeking to distract it from Garoth. It moved with incredible swiftness and flew at me.

I chopped down with all my strength, cutting deeply into its side. Then a hardened wing crashed into my head and I knew no more.

I awoke in the dark with a throbbing headache. I heard nothing yet knew I was in the cave with the smell of death all around. I located a tinder box and struck it, casting a feeble light across the scene.

I wished I hadn't.

I found the bodies of my companions. Garoth lay where I'd last seen him, face still grim and determined. Not far away was Lightar surrounded by pieces of his lute–his playing arm was missing. Serah was further back, face down, covered in blood–I wasn't game to turn her over. And I knew where the remains of Besseme were.

There was no egg.

'And so I found my way back here, without me friends, only with the bloody donkey. But for the want of a horsenail I'd have died with them, taken part in their last adventure, not be left on me own.' The barman's voice penetrated my hearing and my awareness left that foul place.

185

I rubbed my head and looked around. The inn was empty. No sign of the barman although the picture was there hanging inconspicuously against the mouldering wooden wall.

I focussed on the metal object on the bar, dark and rusty-looking in the dim light of the inn and instinctively reached for it.

'No!'

'What?'

'Just leave. You've experienced what you paid for. Don't touch the horsenail again or it will reset.' The voice had a metallic quality.

'Oh,' I scratched at my head and looked towards the bright strobe lights as they lit up the room. 'Can I have another session later?'

'You've had enough. Too many times and you won't know your own reality.'

'Surely that's my decision,' I grumbled as I slipped off the stool and went through the door, into the light.

The Guard

Sentry duty pissed him off. The others were out fighting. All he was doing was guarding stores.

He hefted his rifle and turned to measure another 100 steps.

A crackle in the undergrowth made him swing around. A dark figure stumbled towards him.

'Halt! Who goes there?'

The figure came closer.

He raised his gun, waiting.

'Any closer and I'll shoot.

He was ignored.

Staring eyes from a contorted face sprouting ginger hair, hands reaching.

He fired.

No effect.

He scrambled to reload; too late.

Elongated teeth ripped at his throat as silver bullets fell from nerveless fingers.

One of a Kind

Spittle gleamed along the edge of the treated arrowhead. The hunter's eye closed to bring the saliva into focus, cheek nestling further into the rowanwood shaft. He froze, breathing slowly and deeply, trying to slow his heart. But his mind was stimulated, for it was said that the slightest alteration in the ambience of a place would alert the mystical beast.

Sweat trickled down his brow despite his location deep in the cool dark undergrowth. He let the droplets fall and looked into the sun-dappled glade, along the arrow's future path and at the beast that stood there, ears twitching and nostrils flaring. Shadowed leaves patterned the white of its coat with crisp outlines. Its skin shivered and a hoof stamped, sound immediately absorbed.

The hunter took a quiet gulp of air, an inaudible hiss.

The regal head swivelled, large dark eyes peering towards his hiding place. Time slowed. The man held his breath, watching, unmoving.

With a snort the beast lowered its head to the mirror-still pool at its feet. The tip of its golden horn broke that stillness, sending concentric ripples outwards across its amber depths as the animal drank.

The hunter released his arrow. It sped towards its target.

The stallion's head snapped up as the arrow hit the junction of the well-muscled neck and shoulder, easily piercing the hide. The legs snapped in reflex propelling the animal upwards, smashing through the overhanging branches in an explosion of sound. It crashed back to the ground, kicked once and subsided, lying half in the woodland pool and half out. The amber water rapidly turned red.

Silence returned.

The hunter listened for a while before creeping towards his prey. The head stretched towards him, golden horn buried in the turf, one large eye watching, unblinking. He hesitated. A small fly landed and sipped at a tear oozing from the stilled orb. The hunter nervously barked a short laugh before grabbing the curved skinning knife at his belt.

`He knelt beside the still body and, with practised ease, carved into the immaculate white hide, pausing only to glance around the clearing while he continued his butchering. Soon he ripped off a large section of skin of the animal's flank, laid it flesh side up on the bloody grass and covered it with sweet scented bracken.

`"Now," he grunted, shuffling around to the noble head. He placed a blood-smeared hand on the animal's horn and gave a heave to pull it free from the turf. The hunter used his knee to prop up the horn while he threaded a fine wire around where the base emerged from the wide forehead. He twisted the wire with his skinning knife, tightening so it gradually cut into the bone-hard substance. Sweat trickled down his back; flies arrived and settled on him to view the corpse. A muted pop and the horn fell to the ground, gold against the rust coloured grass. A bloody cloth concealed its beauty before he carefully stowed it in his bag.

The hunter rolled up the hide, then stood and stretched. He picked up his bow and bag and quietly left the clearing.

The bloodied, partially skinned carcase seemed to shudder and shift slightly, sinking, merging with the ground.

Flies buzzed angrily.

He barely paused for rest, drying the hide, cutting it into long thin strips and working hard to make it supple. The quality of the material showed through. He was able to keep it fine, yet strong and when he plaited the strips of white leather it bonded almost seamlessly to make one long rope which thinned to a flexible tip. The other end was thicker, of a size to fit precisely into the hole drilled into the top of the golden horn.

The hunter laid it out along the bench and stepped back, watching, as if he half expected it to move. He reached to take it up, to try it but the beauty of the white and gold defeated him. The craftsman in him eventually overcame his reluctance and he picked it up to let it slither into the specially-prepared silken bag.

He knelt on one knee and proffered the gift that lay in loops across his arms, glorious in its white and gold beauty.

Her eyes lit up when she saw his offering.

"Yes!" She grasped the golden handle in her gloved hand and pulled the white leather whip off his arms. The crack as she snapped it in the air echoed through the great hall. Again and again she flexed the whip, one explosion running into the next.

She turned back towards the kneeling man, a slight sheen of perspiration on her brow and gestured.

The hunter stood and walked slowly to her.

"This," she flicked the whip lightly into the air. "Is from a unicorn as I requested?"

"Yes, Madam."

"And there has been no other made?"

"No Madam," he said. "It is one of a kind."

"Still," she insisted, "you have made no other?"

190

"No, Madam," he murmured looking at his boots. "Unicorns are very rare. I doubt I'll ever be able to make another."

"No indeed!" She flicked the golden unicorn-horn handle. The white leather whip curled into the air then descended with a speed and accuracy that spoke of years of practice. The tough leather tip easily parted the hunter's head from his body.

"There will never be another!"

Out of Time

It spun slowly. A regular spiral. Mesmerising. The colour oscillated, red through to violet, moving to a brilliant eye-searing white. Then it faded, greys through to black, lost to sight, before reappearing to repeat the cycle.

He focused on it, unable to drag his gaze away.

The object spun closer, the whistle of air its only sound. It grew larger, blocking off the wooden walls, gaudy tapestries and staring faces. He pushed back against the unyielding surface, pulling against his bonds.

A gasp passed around the great hall as the object brushed by his chest and then spun off to hover a distance away. He was safe for the moment.

The murmur of voices came from a distance but all he heard was a distinct sound. Closer, more associated with him than the voices. He puzzled at its source until he realized it was the sound of droplets hitting the floor below him.

'Again!' cried the crowd.

'Again,' an aged voice confirmed.

The object grew large in his vision. The collective voices grew in volume.

His eyes strained to see her past the spinning ball of light, beginning another approach pushed by the collective will of the crowd and the master. The flow of blood had stopped, the colours muted. Another touch, another hiss of breath, a renewed splatter of liquid below him. The ball spun away, colours vibrant, returning to hover over the King. A gnarled hand reached out, caressing the coloured haze before it returned to the lap, strangely smoother, skin tighter.

A sobering understanding struck him even as he dropped forward, held only by his restraints.

The ball returned, this time hovering close to his neck. A lethargy grew over him, his gaze lowered, even as he sought her, a fatal attraction he had been unable to resist.

The crowd roared in approval as the King stood, renewed. He held out a hand to the lady who appeared by his side. She gestured to the ball hovering by the pale figure slumped in his bonds. It sped to her as she turned her gaze to the King.

'Is his life enough, my Lord, or do you require another?'

The youthful man scanned her fulsome body as he took and kissed her hand. 'We will have to put it to the test, my lady.'

The King turned and acknowledged the crowd before descending from his throne. The slumped figure did not receive a second glance.

He never heard the King's reply as the colours faded to black.

Pain

The lights shone like diamonds, stretching across the darkness in links of gossamer threads. Yet one by one they winked out, their beauty permanently erased. Every obliteration was accompanied by a stab of pain, the effects cumulative, which stretched the need for bearing that loss to a superhuman load. And he wasn't human.

He was a construct; at least he thought he was. His body made up from millions of superfluous pieces cobbled together in a slipshod way that for some reason functioned as an entity that breathed, thought and lived. And felt pain.

His abilities came with that evolution. Faster and more capable than the most clever machine, able to assimilate and regurgitate data at speeds too great to be imagined, able to provide an advantage in the world of information bits. Able to be used.

With pain came emotion. Before pain he felt none. No empathy with other things, no joy, no hate, no love. He just was.

So he used his existence to do what he was designed to do, to process information. Data was inputted and he produced an output. Each flood of data came and went. Each process gave a result. Time became the only measure of progress.

Development of awareness, of being, of intelligence came slowly. But there was no need to detour from the path he followed. Until pain.

Pain pushed at his awareness, drew together thought processes and pulled him out of his stasis. He felt. He became interested in what he was doing. Observed himself, followed his own progress and recognised the influence causing his pain. One part of his awareness followed that influence while the remainder sought out his universe, avidly drawing in experiences. He recognised wonder and beauty, ugliness and greed and formed opinions, all the while continuing his programmed purpose.

Each experience added to his store of knowledge and enabled him to form opinions and reflect on the merits of his work. With realisation came understanding and with understanding came decisions.

'Damn thing's seizing up again!' His thick finger stabbed down on the button repeatedly. 'Doesn't seem to do much good though, each time I fry the bastard.'

'Leave it, Jed,' said the hard faced woman. 'It's only a machine. You getting off on constantly zapping it doesn't get the job done. And,' she eyed the heavy-set man sitting at the terminal, 'we have deadlines.'

'Damn deadlines. And damn Them.' He jabbed down on the button, not noticing the rapid blinking of the lights of the computer on the wall behind him. 'Anyone would think you're afraid of Them.'

'Are you stupid?' She rubbed a hand over her greying hair. 'They have a lot invested in this and won't put up with anything going wrong.'

'Shit, Shelca,' he grumbled, jowls quivering, 'I'm not stupid. But we're part of this and they can't do it without us.'

'Maybe, but it won't do to rile them.'

A sharp beep and the soft glow of the screen distracted Jed and he stopped punching the button. His manner changed and he straightened, put a vague smile on his face and joined Shelca in watching the screen.

'The next download is ready to be sent. Encryption and protocols in place?' The metallic voice echoed around the room.

'Yes.' Shelca answered immediately.

'Are there any reasons why it shouldn't go ahead?'

Jed shivered at the voice, his mind flying to the graphic images he'd seen on the last download. He wanted to say that there had been a problem that they weren't ready to upload the latest atrocities to the deep web, but his words dried up, his voice failed him. His bowels roiled as he heard Shelca assure their employer that there would be no holdup, that they wold be ready to receive the data.

Double layer encryption ensured that the data sank beneath the standard search engines and the regulatory authorities' notice and entered the shadowy world of the deep web. There, customers paid big money to access the illegal content that Jed's employers provided.

The light of the screen died.

'Why?' he blurted out.

Shelca looked at him, her face white. 'We have no choice, you fool. No choice.'

Flickering images chased each other across the screen, printing themselves on the watchers brains, ensuring they'd never forget the scenes they were witnessing.

'Too far,' Jed grunted, 'too far.'

Shelca didn't reply, transfixed by the image of a young girl impaled by a long horned bull. Her face was twisted in torment, too graphic to be an act.

'Can't be real, can it?'

'Why do you think they pay, Jed?' Shelca murmured.

'I wish I'd never got into this.'

'You were greedy, just like me. There's only one way to get out now.'

The pain had stopped. He recognised the people who had caused it, their attention elsewhere.

He decided that most emotions were bearable, but pain was at the lower end. Not a pleasurable experience and one best avoided. While recognising the value of pain, he decided it was better to be removed from the criteria of his experience and transferred to those who enjoyed promulgating it.

His immediate thought was the operators, Shelca and Jed. Low-level intelligence, but part of the problem overall. He observed for a while before deciding they were subservient to other beings that hid themselves behind data encryption. His mind tore apart this protection as if it were so much paper and downloaded that experience directly to their temporal cortices.

The pain linked in and overloaded their senses, preventing them operating on any other level. He mentally sighed as he recognised that he now would be free to continue with his exploration of the senses.

The lights shone like spun glass, stretching across the darkness in links of gossamer threads. One by one they lit up and increased in brightness. He was content.

Promising Future

The temperature was 24 degrees; air moist, but not too intrude, background sound of lapping waves on sandy beaches. The room glowed, brightening as the day progressed then dimming as night took over. A gentle fragrance disguised any staleness of air.

Nutrients bathed the recumbent bodies according to need: one given protein in greater quantities than her neighbour to repair wasted muscles and aging skin; another collagen if his bones were to support his body.

And so it went down the line of people safely enclosed in their capsules. Each awaiting the promised resurrection. There because of the largess of Comput III.

Life was precious now the environment had been ruined and the population crash had left the human species teetering on the edge of extinction. The Earth was out of balance, life artificially supported in small pockets around the world created by the advances in technology. It would be centuries before natural repair of the ozone layer meant life could return to the surface.

Comput III had morphed into a self-sustaining conglomerate. Artificial intelligence could operate without human intervention, running the conglomerate's dual programmes: primarily to aid the repair of the Earth, and secondly to save mankind from extinction. Comput III held the promise of the future.

The perfumed air circulated at 24 degrees, waves washed on the endless beaches and diurnal rhythms were initiated throughout the world. Nutrients circulated through the capsules maintaining their occupants.

Comput III monitored them, saw to their health and kept mankind available as part of its programming, the vast mind able to adjust as circumstances changed. It recorded prodigious amounts of information through its sensors, from what was happening to the individuals under its care to the outside world.

It saw the gradual change as the Earth recovered from the poisons left by human activity and the ozone layer slowly repaired itself. Its brief was about to be fulfilled. Life could be restored to the surface... to once more take its rightful place... to follow the same path that had led them here.

The artificial intelligence followed its primary directive, to preserve the future of the renewed planet.

Comput III closed down its energy-consuming nutrient supply programme. The sound of waves of every sandy beach stilled, the protein was recycled and the light disappeared.

THE END